Katie's Treasure

PATHFINDER NOVELS

1 *Crispin's Castle,* by Kathleen M. Duncan
2 *Sally and the Shepherdess,* by Kathleen M. Duncan
3 *The Gypsy,* by Janet Kippax
4 *The Wreck of the Pied Piper,* by C. N. Moss
5 *The Runaway Girl,* by Beryl J. Read
6 *Armada Quest,* by Irene Way
7 *Trapped in the Old Cabin,* by Patricia Kershaw
8 *A Truckload of Trouble,* by Patricia Kershaw
9 *The Secret of the Hidden Cave,* by Bettilu D. Davies
10 *Pip's Mountain,* by Beryl J. Read
11 *The Fire Brand,* by Jennifer Rees
12 *Katie's Treasure,* by Eda Stertz

PATHFINDER
NOVEL

Katie's Treasure

EDA STERTZ

ZONDERVAN
PUBLISHING HOUSE
OF THE ZONDERVAN CORPORATION
GRAND RAPIDS, MICHIGAN 49506

KATIE'S TREASURE
by Eda Stertz
© 1980 by The Zondervan Corporation
Grand Rapids, Michigan

ISBN 0-310-37921-0

Edited and designed by Louise H. Rock
Printed in the United States of America

*Written in love
for my grandchildren,
present and future.*

Contents

1 I Know That Treasure's Here 11
2 Caught by the Tide 31
3 Lost in the Woods 51
4 Useful Projects 73
5 Real Indians Lived Here 81
6 When the Detector Goes Beep 91
7 A Super Day 107

1 • I Know
That Treasure's Here

Katie leaned the heavy shovel against her uncle Frank's fence. Lifting the bottom of her T-shirt, she dried the sweat off her face and then off her skinny rib cage.

"I'm going to find that treasure!" she told Lorie.

"Well, I don't think it's even here," Lorie said, throwing down the small spade she'd been digging with. Using the back of her hands, she pushed away the strands of hair curling around her plump face. "We're getting all hot and dirty for nothing. Just like the day we went digging on the beach."

Lorie Gallagher was Katie's best friend, but sometimes she made Katie mad, like right now. Katie looked down at her faded jeans. "What dirt? It's just plain old Florida sand." She tossed her head and her hair flew out like wings on each side of her tanned face. She scowled at Lorie. "That treasure has never been found, so it has got to be right here in this backyard."

Lorie glared back at her. "Maybe it never was here. Right?"

"Wrong! It was buried here and it's still here." Grabbing the shovel again, Katie started digging in a different place.

Her uncle Frank didn't care how many holes she dug in his yard. He'd lived alone in the house since her grandmother Reise died. The only thing special he ever did about the yard was to pay a neighborhood boy to cut down the weeds in her grandmother's old flower beds.

"Just you keep digging," Katie ordered.

Lorie groaned as if Katie had told her to go jump off the bluff, but she picked up her spade and slowly began turning the hot gray sand over in a small heap at her feet.

Katie frowned again when she heard her grandmother Bradbury calling her. This grandmother had moved back here to the island to live with them last winter when Katie's mother started working with her father at their hardware store.

Grandmother Bradbury was supposed to look after the house and take care of Katie. Katie thought she took the last part of her job much too seriously. After all, Katie wasn't exactly a child! She was eleven years old, nearly. How much looking after did she need?

Watching Grandmother round the corner of the house, Katie sighed, knowing she was in for a scolding. Her grandmother's hair, usually perfectly in place, was sticking out in little wisps and she was dripping with perspiration.

"Kathryn Bradbury Reise! What are you doing over here? You are supposed to be at Lorie's house practicing your piano duet for the recital."

12

Katie stopped shoveling and wiped her face again, this time with her arm. "We know that old piece by heart, Grandmother. So does Lorie's mother. She ran us out of the house."

"But she didn't mean for you to take on a project like this. Do you want to have a heat stroke? And look at you! You're filthy! My goodness, Katie B., you're nearly eleven. Can't you grow up a little?"

Katie folded in her lips stubbornly and stared down at the new hole she'd been digging. That had been a pretty unfair thing for her grandmother to say. Her other grandmother would never have said it. She would have understood that Katie wanted nothing more than to grow up. She could hardly wait to get on with important things like going to high school and being a cheerleader and getting her driver's license.

Katie couldn't understand how her two grandmothers could be so different in their looks and ways. This grandmother was short, and although not fat, she was getting pretty close to it. She kept her hair frosted so Katie didn't know how gray it might be, and wore make-up matched to her skin in a beauty parlor. The plastic rims of her glasses were the same soft blue as her eyes.

Her grandmother Reise hadn't cared very much for matched make-up or regular schedules. Her dark hair was clearly going gray and her skin was brown and wrinkled from working in her yard. She might decide to weave a macrame plant hanger in the morning, while other women were doing things like waxing their kitchen floors. Then she'd wax her floor after the others had gone to bed. Or she might put down her macrame and say to Katie, "It's such a beautiful day. Let's go see what's blooming in the woods!" She told the best stories of any grandmother in town and baked the best oatmeal cookies of anybody in the whole world.

She died of cancer when Katie was nine years old. Katie had stopped crying for her, but she had not stopped missing her. Sometimes Katie thought her grandmother Bradbury had been brought here to take her other grandmother's place. Whenever she thought this, she got angry! Angry at her mother for not understanding her better, and especially angry at her grandmother.

Lorie was blushing as she always did when she was in trouble with grownups. She dusted the sand off her spade with her fingertips. "We were just going to dig a little until suppertime," she said, as if she thought she'd better apologize.

Katie's grandmother sighed. "But it is much too hot here in the sun." She sighed again. "And besides, you're just wasting time."

Katie looked up. "That's not true. Gran'ma Reise told me to keep digging. She told me there really is treasure here. Uncle Frank says so too."

Her grandmother looked sad, as she always did when Katie talked about Gran'ma Reise. She shrugged her shoulders. "Well, I want you home in twenty minutes. You'll have to take a shower before supper. Lorie doesn't even look dirty."

Katie tossed her head, sending her hair flying again. "That's because I'm the serious digger. Lorie just stirs the sand around like a little old doodlebug."

● ● ● ● ●

After supper Katie's mother and father went off to visit friends. Katie thought the least they could have done was to go to a movie and take her. But no, it was a school night and besides, her mother said there wasn't anything on that was fit for decent folks to see.

Katie definitely felt sorry for herself. It seemed that since her mother started working, the family hardly ever did anything fun together. She stretched out on the couch in the family room, thinking she might just sulk until they got back.

Katie had gotten involved in one of her favorite shows on television when her grandmother came in. "Katie, what about your homework? Are you all finished?"

Katie didn't look up immediately. Couldn't her grandmother see she was interrupting an interesting part?

Her grandmother sat down, picked up her needle-point, and began making her careful stitches across the brown canvas.

Feeling a little ashamed of herself, Katie said, "Oh, I'm sorry, Grandmother. What were you saying?"

"I think you know I was asking you about your homework. I don't understand your watching television on a school night, especially here at the end of the year when you ought to be concentrating on finishing up well."

"I don't have any homework. I did all the written junk in homeroom and the only other thing I have to do is tell a true story about Florida in history class. That's easy. I'm going to tell about the treasure buried in Uncle Frank's backyard."

Her grandmother frowned as Katie knew she would. "But Katie, dear. The treasure story isn't Florida history. It's only a kind of legend. One of your uncle's tall tales."

"And Gran'ma Reise's. She told me first. And it's not a tall tale. It's true."

Her grandmother shook her head. "Don't blame me if Miss Thomas gives you a bad grade."

"She won't. She's pretty neat about things like that. Anyway, I'm going to tell it." She looked back at the television so she wouldn't see her grandmother shaking her head.

• • ● • •

Standing in front of her history class, Katie was eager to tell her story.

"Once there was this weird old man, see? He was kind of scary looking, with black hair down in long braids like an Indian and skin burnt brown as leather by the sun. He lived all by himself in a beat-up old shack in the woods."

"Petey Moon!" the kids yelled.

"Not Petey Moon, you dum-dums. This was a long time ago, even before our grandparents were born. Anyway, this old man was a beggar. He pushed a cart with squeaky wheels and he begged for bread and looked in other people's trash piles for junk to haul off in his cart."

Katie lowered her voice and leaned forward. "Sometimes in the night you could hear the squeaky wheels going by in the street. And sometimes they'd stop and you knew who was in your yard. Little kids were scared to death because parents were always saying,

'Old man Domingo gonna get you if you're bad.' "

Miss Thomas spoke up. "Katie, we're not telling ghost stories, you know."

Katie stepped back a little. "Sorry, I just got carried away." She looked at the class. "Anyway, this old guy acted like he didn't have any money at all, that he had to beg for everything he needed. But just before he died, he told a man that he'd buried a lot of money in a secret place right in town."

Miss Thomas held up a hand to stop her, but Katie hurried on. She had the kids' full attention, although many of them had heard the story before.

"The old man said the treasure was buried where three trees were growing together in a triangle. A magnolia, a pine, and a cedar. The branches of the trees came together in an arch. The treasure was buried in the center of that arch, not too deep, not too shallow."

Katie paused a moment and one of the kids who had just moved to the island asked, "And then what happened?"

"Then the old man died, and everybody in town started looking for those three trees. They looked all over town and there was only one such triangle—and it was in my great-great-grandfather's backyard!"

She folded her arms in triumph, but in just a moment she dropped them and hurried on before Miss Thomas could interrupt. "My great-great-grandfather dug, and his children dug. They dug inside the triangle and all around, but they couldn't find a thing. And then other people paid my great-great-grandfather to let them dig, but nobody ever found the treasure."

17

"Can I go dig there?" the new kid asked.

Katie grinned smugly. "Sure. I don't care."

Miss Thomas rapped on her desk. "All right now. I think we'll have to finish this up. Katie, that wasn't really what I had in mind when I asked for historical stories."

"Right, Miss Thomas, but can I say one more thing?"

"If it's a short thing."

"It's short. I just want to say why I don't care who digs there. I believe the reason none of the people looking have ever found the treasure is because the Lord hasn't meant them to find it." She grinned widely at the class. "And I think I'm the one He means to find it. And I'm going to—you wait and see!"

The kids hooted at that and one of them said, "Oh, yeah, when? You've been digging since you got your first sand bucket."

Katie shrugged. "Don't worry. I'll find it. Maybe this afternoon."

• • ● • •

Katie had just gotten home from school when her mother stopped by the house on her way to the beauty shop. The only time she ever went there was when she needed a haircut. Her hair was super-curly and she liked to wear it short and shaped to her head like a little cap.

Katie sometimes wished she'd inherited her mother's shiny blond curls, but then in the next minute she was glad she'd gotten her grandmother Reise's thick hair instead. Of course, it was her father's hair too, but his was thin on top.

Before Katie could tell her mother what she wanted to do that afternoon, her mother said, "I don't want you to go over to your uncle Frank's house any more unless some of us are with you. There's all kind of traffic on that street now and Petey Moon hangs around whenever he's in town."

"Oh, Mamma! Uncle Frank says Petey's never done anything bad. He's just kind of weird, that's all."

"Nobody's ever proved he did anything bad, but he's always being picked up on suspicion of one thing or another. Don't argue with me, Katie. Just do as I say. I don't want to have to worry about you when I'm at work."

Katie scowled. "I wish you didn't go to work at all."

"I'm working to help pay for this house and so you can go to college."

Katie tossed her head. "I'm not going to college. I'm going to be an oceanographer."

"You have to go to college to be an oceanographer, silly." She picked up her things to go, but Katie caught her hand.

"Let's talk about college and what I'd have to study to be an oceanographer."

Her mother hugged her a moment. "I can't right now, Katie B. I'm late for my appointment and then I have to go back to the store. Talk to your grandmother. She's out in the patio swing."

Katie frowned again. "She doesn't know about anything interesting. I wish—I wish—"

Her mother shook her head and her gray-green eyes were sad. "It's no use wishing, Katie. Your grandmother Reise was truly a wonderful person, but she's been dead nearly two years now. You have just got to accept that." She sighed. "You ought to be grateful to the Lord that you had her as long as you did, and that now she's gone, you have another grandmother to love you and help take care of you. If you'd just give her half a chance you'd find out my mother is a pretty wonderful person, too."

Katie pushed away from her mother. "But she can't take Gran'ma's place!" she cried, half in anger, half in tears.

Her mother caught her in her arms again. "Oh, Katie, I didn't mean it that way. Of course, nobody can take Gran'ma Reise's place. You'll always remember her and love her. But, don't you see? Your gran'ma Reise wouldn't want you to keep on missing her so much that you shut out other people."

"Like Grandmother?"

"Of course, like Grandmother."

Katie heaved her shoulders in a big sigh. "Well, okay, I'll try. But I wish she wouldn't be so strict. I wish she'd ease up on me a little."

Her mother gave her a little shove, but she was smiling. "I've really got to run," she said.

Katie caught her hand. "Could you take me over to Uncle Frank's for a little while tonight?"

Her mother shook her head. "I can't tonight. Dad and I are cleaning out the storeroom after we close up. I'm sure Mamma will take you if you ask her nicely." She gave Katie a quick good-by wave and hurried out the door.

Katie went into the family room and flopped on the couch. No need to ask her grandmother, even nicely.

She would just say that the gnats were too bad on the river in the evening, or something dumb like that. But then, Katie thought of a neat new place to dig, so she decided to ask her anyway, just in case.

"Well, I was going to write letters tonight," her grandmother said, "but I guess I could do them when we get back." Katie clapped her hands together and her grandmother said, "Why don't you invite Lorie for supper and afterwards we'll go over and you can dig until it gets dark."

• • ● • •

Supper wasn't ready yet when Lorie came. Katie grabbed the Frisbee. "Hey, let's go out and throw a few."

They hadn't sailed it more than a couple of times when Katie's grandmother came out on the patio.

"Katie, dear, why are you playing with that thing out here?"

"There's nothing else to do, Grandmother."

"But that's for playing with at the beach or the park. It could go out in the street or you could break a window."

"Oh, Grandmother, don't be so nervous all the time. We're throwing it very easy and we're not going to break anything. See?"

She raised her arm and sent the Frisbee sailing across the yard. Just because her grandmother was watching, it took a sudden dip, curved, and smacked right into one of the rose bushes in the corner. The bush trembled and petals and tiny green sprouts went flying through the air.

Katie put her hand to her mouth. "Oops, I'm sorry, Grandmother. I hope it didn't hurt it or anything."

Her grandmother rushed out to the rose bed to examine the bush and Katie followed. There weren't any major branches broken, but her grandmother tamped down the soil and mulch around the bush and talked to it as if it were a person. "Poor thing, you almost got knocked out of the ground." She bent to pick up the Frisbee and turned to Katie. "No more throwing this thing in the yard, you hear? I will not have you tearing up my roses."

"Yes, ma'am, I hear, and I won't," Katie said, feeling relieved. She had been afraid her grandmother was so angry she wouldn't take them to Uncle Frank's.

● ● ● ● ●

It was cooler digging with the sun gone down behind the trees across the river, but that was the only thing that was easier about this try. The soft Florida sand was powdery dry and sifted back into the hole they were digging almost as fast as they could lift it out. They kept working, but at near dark they had turned up only a rusty tin can and some pieces of sea shell bleached white as chalk.

Lorie said, "Oh, Katie, let's quit. I'm tired of looking for this silly treasure. I'd rather go home and watch television."

That made Katie angry so she started digging harder than ever. She wouldn't let Lorie give up until it was too dark to see what they were doing.

Starting toward the swing, Katie whispered fiercely, "Don't mention going home. I want to hear Uncle Frank talk."

Katie thought her uncle seemed younger than her father, although he was older. Maybe this was because her father dressed up in a suit and shirt to go to work every day and to church twice on Sunday. The only time Katie had seen her uncle dressed up, or at church, was when he went to her grandmother's funeral two years ago.

He had dark brown hair like his mother's had been, except his was curly and had just the tiniest bit of gray in front of his ears. He squinted his dark eyes a lot, making you think he couldn't see, but mostly he was just laughing or closing his eyes against the sun. He was always tan from being out in the sun fishing or painting houses.

He didn't go to work at a regular job because he'd been wounded in Vietnam and drew a pension. His mother had willed him the old family home after Katie's father built their new one. Uncle Frank fished a lot for his own pleasure and occasionally he took people out on his boat. He painted houses when he got low on cash.

Katie thought he was the neatest possible uncle to have. At times she almost wished he were her father. She didn't allow herself to wish it all the way because she thought that would be a sin.

Katie unfolded a plastic chair by the swing and sat down next to him.

"No treasure yet?" he asked.

"Not yet. I think I'll look for a different one for a while. Tell me about another one. How about the one in the woods behind the old fort?"

"Oh, Frank, please don't," her grandmother said.

"Can't you divert the child to some more practical project?"

He laughed. "What could be more practical than hunting treasure?"

"I'd rather watch TV," Lorie said.

Uncle Frank gave the swing a gentle push. "Well, the treasure story that you're talking about is not necessarily true. Just like the story about the treasure here in our yard is not necessarily completely true."

Katie started to protest but he interrupted her. "Don't get your hackles up. I've heard both those old tales all my life and as far as I'm concerned they're true, or at least there's some truth in them. The treasure in the woods back of the fort is supposed to have been buried in the early 1800s when there were lots of pirates in these parts. The fort wasn't there then. It wasn't built until around the time of the Civil War.

"Anyway, the story goes that this particular pirate, we called him Blackbeard when we were kids, came ashore up near where the fort is now with a chest full of Spanish gold. He brought two or three men and a cabin boy with him to carry the treasure. They walked a little way along the beach and then cut back up into the woods to find a good, safe place. When Blackbeard found just the spot he wanted, he ordered the men to dig a deep hole and let down the chest. Then he ordered them to cover it over and pile leaves and branches all around it."

"Did they mark it so they could find it again?" Katie asked, moving closer to her uncle. She already knew the whole story, but she liked to hear every part just the same way every time.

"Sure, that old skunk marked it all right. He chained the cabin boy to the nearest tree and told him he was to guard the treasure until he came back for it. Then he just up and shot him, and left his ghost to do the guarding."

Katie gasped as she always did at that part of the story.

"Ugh," her grandmother said. "I never did like that story. And you know there's no such thing as ghosts."

"Grandmother! You're ruining the whole thing!"

"I'm sorry about that, Katie, but there really aren't any ghosts."

"Of course not," her uncle said, "but the ghost is a part of the story. Anyway, old Blackbeard never found the treasure chest again and neither did any of the other pirates. When they came back with shovels, thinking they knew just where it was, they couldn't find it. Nobody else has found it either, though many a man has tried. It's always same. If you haven't got anything to dig with, you might find the tree with the chain hanging on it. If you go back for a shovel you'll never find the tree again, even if you drop things to make a trail."

"What happens to the things you drop?" Lorie asked, twisting one curl around her finger the way she did whenever she was feeling uneasy about something.

"Well, I guess the boy's ghost just takes them away or something," said Uncle Frank.

Katie's grandmother shook her head, and Uncle Frank shrugged.

"I know, Mary Ruth," he said, "and it's just a story, but lots of people have believed it. You probably did yourself when you were growing up on the island. I not only believed it, I looked for the plagued treasure."

Katie had never heard him admit this before. She grabbed both his arms. "Did you ever find the chain?"

"No, but a fisherman friend of mine swears he did."

"I believe him," Katie said, tightening her grip on his arms. "Would you take me to look for it? I'll figure someway to outsmart that ghost."

He threw back his head, laughing, and then he looked at her. "Oh, Katie. I might take you. I just might."

Katie sat back in her chair, her high hopes fading. When a grownup said "might" you could usually put it down for a "no."

Lorie had put her hands over her ears. "Will you all hush up about ghosts? You're going to give me bad dreams."

"Oh, who's afraid of bad dreams?" Katie scoffed. "Let's talk some more about pirates, Uncle Frank."

• • ● • •

Katie turned and twisted in her bed. She knew she was having a nightmare but she couldn't wake herself up. In her dream she and Lorie had gone to the woods to look for the tree with the chain wrapped around it. Then she had become the cabin boy chained to the tree. Old Captain Blackbeard was stomping the sand down over the buried chest and telling his men how he was going to kill her so her ghost would guard the treasure.

Katie tried to signal Lorie to come unhook the chain before the captain came back, but Lorie was watching TV and wouldn't even turn her head to look at Katie.

26

Then the captain came walking toward her with his long arms reaching for her throat. "Help, Lorie! He's going to choke me. Help, Mamma! Grandmother! Anybody!"

She strained at the chain. Blackbeard grabbed her shoulder and began to shake her.

"Katie, Katie! Wake up! wake up! You're having a nightmare."

Katie pushed at the hands and sat up in bed, her eyes straining awake. Her grandmother was standing by her bed. "Captain Blackbeard almost killed me," Katie cried.

Her grandmother sat down and put her arms around her. "It was only a bad dream, dear. He's gone back to the land of make-believe, and you're safe in your own bed."

Katie relaxed against her grandmother a minute and then pushed away, although she was still a little frightened. "I'm okay. I'm not a little baby, you know."

"Of course you aren't. Everybody has bad dreams that scare them, even grownups." Grandmother straightened Katie's sheet, which had gotten all twisted around her body. "You'll be fine now." Picking up the rag doll that had fallen off Katie's bed, she said, "Here, hold Lady Jane for a few minutes. She's had quite a scare herself."

Katie's other grandmother had made the Victorian-style doll for Katie a long time ago. Her embroidered eyes dropped and her mouth had a little halfway smile. Her dark brown yarn hair was parted in the middle and covered by a lace-trimmed bonnet. She was wearing a stiff dress with lots of tiny pleats and lace. Black shoes peeped out below the long skirt. Katie adored her.

Katie took the doll, but spoke crossly to her grandmother. "Stop talking to me as if I was a baby. And besides, I'm much too old for dolls. I only keep Lady Jane on my bed for decoration."

Her grandmother stood up to leave. "Of course. But there's nothing wrong with loving dolls, you know, at any age. When you're too old to play with them you can collect them and enjoy them as long as you live." She looked around at all the dolls sitting on shelves and in chairs. "You're using quite a lot of them for decoration in here. Actually, you have a good start at a collection already."

She reached to turn off the lamp. "Would you like me to pray with you, and ask God to help you go back to sleep and not have any more bad dreams?"

"I'd rather pray by myself."

"All right, dear, but I'll pray for you too, back in my room." She started out, then turned back. "One of these days when there's time I'll tell you a treasure story that isn't frightening."

Katie's mouth flew open. "You know a treasure story?"

Her grandmother laughed. "Yes, I do. Remember, I grew up here, too, and heard all the tales your father and uncle Frank heard and now you're hearing."

"Gran'ma Reise was the main one to tell me stories," Katie said. She didn't say it, but she was sure this grandmother could never tell such good ones.

Her grandmother sighed. "I know she did, Katie.

She always loved anything that was dramatic or adventurous." She sighed again. "You forget, dear. Janie and I were good friends when we were growing up."

"I don't understand that," Katie said. "You're not at all alike."

"No, but you and Lorie aren't much alike either."

Katie thought a minute. "That's true," she said. "Tell me the story now!"

"Oh, no, I won't. You've had enough stories for one day. You have your prayer time with God now so you can go on to sleep. I'll tell you something else though. After you went to bed tonight your mother said that she wanted us all to do something together this weekend. She's thinking we could go to the beach late Saturday afternoon and take a picnic supper. How does that sound to you?"

"Great! Can Lorie go?"

"I'm sure that will be all right with us if it's all right with her parents."

Katie wasn't sure it was safe to feel happy about the prospects of the whole family going on a picnic. "Did Daddy say he would go?"

"Yes. He said you and I could go early to swim if we liked. He and your mother will come later, for our picnic supper."

Katie sank down in her bed and then she sat back up again. "Do you really know a treasure story?" she asked.

"Just wait and see," her grandmother said.

2 · Caught by the Tide

If Katie hadn't had a Girls' Mission Club meeting at church she probably would have worried the treasure story out of her grandmother in nothing flat. Instead she and Lorie walked slowly toward the church, talking about going to the beach tomorrow, and what kind of refreshments Mrs. Bailey would come up with today.

Mrs. Bailey was not one of Katie's favorite people, and she had to listen to her teach both in Sunday school and at Club. Katie's mother had told her several times that since Mrs. Bailey had never had any children of her own she might expect too much of the girls, but that she certainly meant well. "Just appreciate her for giving so much time to you children," her mother said.

Katie appreciated her most for her refreshments. She was pretty good at that. Maybe today they'd have brownies.

"Do you know your part in the program?" Lorie asked.

"Naturally," Katie said. "I always know my part in the program, don't I? Especially since my grandmother lives with us. She reminds me. Honestly, she's nearly as bad as Mrs. Bailey."

"Oh, Katie, she's not. Not nearly. At least she doesn't call you 'Precious.' "

Katie giggled, because Lorie had mimicked Mrs. Bailey's high, sweet voice perfectly.

They were passing a wide vacant lot and both stopped when they saw something unusual going on. Two utility trucks had pulled in off the street. Several men in bright orange jackets and hard hats were in the field. A couple of them had shovels and were following another man with a metal box in his hand. A long staff reached from the box down to the ground where it was attached to something that looked like a plate. The man was pushing the plate slowly along the ground.

"He's got a metal detector," Lorie said. "I've seen them on TV."

"I know what it is," Katie said, "but what's he doing with it in this lot?"

Lorie shrugged, and Katie caught her hand. "Let's go see."

Lorie pulled back.

"Come on silly. I just recognized the guy with the detector. He's Bud Williams and he sings in our choir. I'm going to ask him what he's doing."

When Lorie didn't move, Katie started toward the men by herself. Lorie reluctantly followed.

"Hi, Bud," Katie said. "What's happening?"

He looked around. "Oh, hi, Katie. Nothing much. The building over there is having a plumbing problem.

It may originate in some old pipes here. We don't know where the pipes are, exactly, so we're using this detector. Saves a lot of digging."

"Wow! Will that thing really find the pipes?" Katie asked.

"Sure. And anything else metal, unfortunately." He pointed in back of them to a small heap of old tin cans and other pieces of rusted metal.

"That's really neat," Katie said. "Can we watch?"

He didn't answer immediately and Lorie pulled at her arm. "Come on, Katie. We've got to go to church. We'll be late."

"No we won't. We've got time to watch for a little while. Can we, Bud?"

He shrugged and grinned at the other men. "I guess, but stay back out of our way."

Katie tried to do that and see what he was doing at the same time. The plate slid along unevenly over the grass and weeds making a steady, humming sound. Then it began to hum much louder.

"It's found something," Katie said, excited.

He nodded and stepped back. One of the men came up and lifted out a heavy shovel full of dirt and weeds. Another tin can fell to the ground. Bud threw it aside and moved ahead.

A few minutes later the detector signaled metal again and the man began digging at that spot. This time it was different. He hit what he thought was a pipe. Both men dug together, lifting out great shovels full of dirt and opening up a perfectly splendid hole. Katie clapped her hands and wished she had a shovel.

"*Katie*," Lorie said, moving farther back out of the

way. "We have to go. Come on now. Mrs. Bailey will be upset."

"Just a few more minutes, Lorie. It's just getting interesting."

"Well, I'm going," Lorie said. "You can stay here and get in trouble if you want to."

• • ● • •

Katie's mother was on her way to the bank to make a deposit when she passed the vacant lot where the men were working. She slowed down in amazement because she thought she saw Katie standing between them. And then Katie disappeared. Mrs. Reise braked her car at the curb just as one of the men threw down his shovel and kneeled beside the pile of dirt he had dug up.

It was only about five minutes later that Katie was in the ladies' room at the church getting washed up. Her mother had delivered her there with a few sharp words and the promise of a few more later.

Sliding into a chair next to Lorie, Katie whispered, "You missed all the excitement. I stepped too close to where the men were digging and fell slap-dab in the hole."

Mrs. Bailey said, "Let's not whisper, girls. Katie, it's past time for your part in the program, but we'll fit it in somehow. And then we have to work on our missionary scrapbooks and practice saying our Scripture passages for our Recognition Service at church next month."

"Yes, ma'am," Katie said. "I'm ready whenever you are."

• • ● • •

Refreshments did include brownies and Mrs. Bailey gave Katie three, even though she scolded her for being late. "It's a matter of courtesy," she said, "and behaving courteously is just another way of being kind."

"And the Bible says, 'Be ye kind,' " Katie said, knowing Mrs. Bailey would say that next.

In spite of the scolding, Katie enjoyed the meeting, especially the part about missionaries in faraway places. Walking home with Lorie she said, "I might be a foreign missionary when I grow up. If God calls me to do it."

"Well, I might be a home missionary," Lorie said, "so I wouldn't get mixed up in revolutions and bombings."

Katie scowled at her. "That's being a coward. Wouldn't you be willing to face danger if it meant you could talk to people about God?"

Lorie stopped walking, put her hands on her hips, and faced Katie. "Maybe I'm a coward, but I think you're more interested in the danger than in telling people about God. Lots of people right here in Oclonee don't really understand about God and how he loves them and wants them to live. Like your uncle Frank, for instance. He never goes to church and I've heard some things about him that don't sound too great."

"Just leave my uncle out of this, will you?"

"But you shouldn't leave him out of it. He's a part of your family. We ought to feel responsible for our families as much as for people way off in Africa."

Katie tossed her head. "Mrs. Bailey! Mrs. Bailey! I'm sick of old lady Bailey!"

Lorie looked as if she might cry. "Katie, sometimes you don't even act like a Christian."

Katie stared at Lorie angrily. It was mean of her to talk so about Uncle Frank, and it was mean of her to say Katie didn't act like a Christian. That was what the Bible called judging. Katie started to fire back something mean herself, but turned away instead. Because mean or not, the things Lorie had said were true.

She began walking on toward home, Lorie close behind. Neither said anything until they got to the place where the men had been working with the detector. She whirled toward Lorie. "If I just had one of those metal detectors I could find the treasure in Uncle Frank's backyard in nothing flat!"

• • ● • •

Katie and her grandmother picked Lorie up at three o'clock on Saturday. They drove out to the beach and then along the stretch of hard-packed sand near the water's edge. They were going down to the south end of the island where there wouldn't be much traffic.

Katie's parents planned to come soon after five when they closed up the store. Her father didn't get too excited about picnics—he'd rather eat a good seafood dinner at a restaurant—but once in a great while he'd agree to go to the beach with his family. Sometimes he'd even make a bonfire so they could roast hot dogs and marshmallows.

If the tide was right, he might take his rod and reel and wade out in the surf to make a few casts. He said he did this just to keep in practice in case he ever had time to go on a real fishing trip.

Today the tide would be high before dark and there

36

wouldn't be time for a bonfire. Her father would want to get the cars up off the beach while there was still a strip of hard-packed sand to drive along.

The girls already had on their bathing suits under their shorts, but today Katie didn't have swimming on her mind. She waited for her grandmother to get settled in a yellow plastic chair near the water, and then she demanded, "Now tell us the treasure story!"

Her grandmother scolded a little. "Katie, don't be so impatient. Don't you want to swim first while it's still hot?"

"Yes, we do," Lorie said, beginning to peel off her shorts.

Katie grabbed her arm and pulled her back. "No, first we want to hear the story."

Her grandmother laughed. "Don't worry, Lorie, it's only a little story."

Katie thought, I'll bet it is, and a dumb one too. But she sat down on the wet sand by her grandmother's chair and, after a moment, Lorie sat down too.

Katie's grandmother hesitated. "Well, I can't say how much of it is true. I heard it as a child, but I know it has some basis in fact."

"Go on, go on," Katie said.

"A long time ago a man was walking out along the beach—"

"Where on the beach?" Katie interrupted. "Here where we are, or down at the other end?"

"I'm not really sure. I think it was down here on the south end."

"Good."

"Anyway, one day after an unusually high tide he

was walking up close to the dunes and he saw a brick. Well, that was a little unusual because there were no brick houses on the beach at that time, in fact, no houses at all where he was walking. He reasoned the brick must have been part of the ballast of a ship. Maybe there had been a shipwreck a long time ago or, for some reason, the brick had been tossed overboard and had gradually washed in. So he went on walking and in just a little while he saw another brick. It lay parallel to the ocean just like the first one. This was really strange. He walked on faster, and sure enough, he came to another brick, parallel to the beach just like the other two, and all at the same distance from each other and from the dunes.

"He thought then that he must be following some sort of trail. When he'd come on several more bricks identically placed, he was sure of it!

"Then he ran out of the bricks. He walked a long way but he couldn't find any more bricks. So he went back to the last one he had found. Again he stopped to reason. There were no visible bricks out to the water. It wouldn't have done any good to place the bricks going out to the water because the changing tides would have covered them up or washed them away. Even up here close to the dunes he wouldn't have seen the bricks if last night's full-moon tide hadn't washed the soft sand away from them."

Katie was up on her knees and staring into her grandmother's face. "The trail went up between the dunes," she said.

"Yes, it did," said Grandmother. "Walking up through a trough between two dunes, he counted off

the approximate number of feet there had been between the other bricks. At first he couldn't find anything, but he got down on his hands and knees and
began to dig in a wide circle in the soft, hot sand."

She paused.

"And?" Katie and Lorie asked at once.

"He found a brick."

The girls both sighed their relief and she went on.
"He followed the same procedure through the dunes
and into the oak hummock on the other side. And then
he came to a little fresh-water lake and at its edge he
found the last brick, in fact he found three bricks together pointed in toward each other. He knew that
under those bricks there had to be something mighty
interesting."

"There had to be," Lorie said. "Maybe even a dead
person."

"You hush," Katie said. "He certainly didn't find a
plain old dead person."

Her grandmother went on. "Well, he didn't know
what might be buried there, but he knew he had to find
out. It was already late and he didn't have a shovel, so
he'd have to come back the next day."

Katie groaned. "Oh, it's not going to be like the
chain treasure!"

Her grandmother shook her head. "No. He went
back to the beach, stared at the dunes and the oak
hummock until he'd memorized exactly where he'd
gone into the woods. Then he went along the beach
and covered up all the bricks."

"So nobody else could find them," Lorie said.

"Yes, and the next day he came back with his horse

and buggy and a shovel and dug up the ground under the bricks by the lake."

"What'd he find?" the girls cried together.

"He found a chest of gold coins and gold bars. It had probably been buried there by pirates no telling how many years before."

"A real pirate treasure," said Katie with a satisfied sigh.

"Yes, and a big one. The man knew if the government discovered he'd found it, he'd have to turn over a large share. So he told only a few friends and then skipped the country."

Katie said, "You mean you have to give the government part of a treasure if you find one?"

"Yes, and if it's something old and historical, the government is especially interested in your find."

Lorie shook her head. "He should have just given the government its share and stayed home to enjoy the rest."

Katie said, "Oh, no. He was smart. I'll do the same thing he did when I find my treasure. I'm going to keep it every bit, even if I have to run away."

"In that case I hope you never find one," her grandmother said.

Katie stared at her a moment and then got up and started toward the water.

Her grandmother got up too and caught her arm.

"I don't really mean I don't want you to find a treasure. But you sounded so terribly selfish, as if having a lot of gold would be the most important thing in the world to you. Besides, I'd hate to think of your leaving home."

Katie shrugged. "It's okay. I know what you meant. And thanks for the story. I liked it a lot."

She turned to Lorie, who had gotten a towel from the car and was carefully folding it over the arm of the plastic chair. "Come on, slowpoke, I thought you wanted to go swimming!"

• • ● • •

When Katie's parents were late coming, her grandmother let Katie and Lorie go ahead and eat. They thought they might starve if they had to wait any longer. There was crisp fried chicken, potato salad with lots of eggs and pickles, wedges of tomato and lettuce, fruit salad, and fat slices of pound cake.

"Wow!" Katie said, finishing off the last crumb on her plate. "I'm full as a tick."

"What a dreadful expression," her grandmother said.

"Yeah. Have you ever seen a full tick?"

"Never mind," her grandmother said hastily.

Katie got up to put her things in the trash bag. "While we're waiting for Mom and Dad, Lorie and I want to take a walk."

"Now, Katie," her grandmother said. "I don't think there are any more bricks to follow."

"I don't think so either, but you can't tell for sure. Besides, I've got some new ideas on things to look for now. For instance, you might find driftwood in a trail."

"Dum-dum," Lorie scoffed. "Driftwood would have washed away or rotted by now."

"Dum-dum, yourself. Don't you know there are old ship hulls under the water that have been there for years and years? Uncle Frank says so. And driftwood stays dry in the sun and air and lasts forever."

Lorie made a scornful sound. "Any pirate stupid enough to mark his treasure with driftwood is too stupid to have a very big treasure."

"Oh, come now, girls, don't spoil the day with a quarrel. Take a walk, but don't go very far. The tide is coming in, Katie, and your daddy will want to get the cars off the beach before the water gets much higher."

"We promise, we promise!" Katie cried, off in a run.

• • ● • •

An hour later Katie's mother and father had finished their supper. Katie's father was fussing because the girls weren't back yet.

He took off his thick-framed glasses to polish them with his handkerchief. Putting them back on again, he stared at his mother-in-law, his brown eyes and wide mouth serious. "I wish you hadn't let them go off," he said to her.

"But I told them not to go too far."

"Well, they've obviously done just that, gone too far." He had been sitting in the dry sand just above the tide line watching the long, curling waves roll in. Now he put on his tennis shoes and stood up, his tall body casting a shadow behind him. "Well, maybe there's no harm done. I'll go down the beach and get them." He hesitated. "I don't know whether to take the car or walk."

"Maybe you ought to take the car," his wife said. "They're still not in sight. You can get to them and back a lot faster than if you walk. You've still got a little hard sand to drive on."

He nodded, got in the car, and started the motor. Then he leaned out the window. "Kathryn, you and Mary Ruth go on down the beach now to the first approach and get up on the parking lot. I should be back there with the girls soon if Katie hasn't gone clean to the end of the island!"

• • ● • •

"We're almost at the end!" Katie cried out in delight, spotting the rounded curve ahead where the sand seemed to disappear into the ocean. "And there's a tremendous pile of driftwood. Come on, let's go!"

This was the most exciting thing they'd found since the big palm tree that had washed up on the beach. The tree was stretched across the hard sand, its root ball in the water, its drying fronds up in the soft sand near the dunes.

They played there a few minutes, jumping flat footed across it a couple of times, and even shoving at it to see if they could get it back into the water to float. But it was much too heavy for them to budge.

Then they'd walked some more, running up into the soft sand every few minutes to inspect a clump of sea weeds, the remains of a bonfire, dead crab shells and fish, and then back to the water to scuff their feet through the foamy edge of the incoming waves.

Katie reached this new pile of rotting boards first. She pulled at one board that was sticking up in the air. "This may be it! There's probably a cache of gold coins right under this wood."

"You are really crazy," Lorie said, but she helped Katie pull.

The board's other end was buried deep in the sand

and it wouldn't come out. Katie fell to her knees and began digging with both hands.

Lorie watched her. "Who would bury treasure this close to the water?"

Katie kept digging. "This old wood could be from some Spanish galleon that got wrecked in a hurricane. And part of it has finally washed to shore."

"That sounds pretty reasonable," Lorie said and started digging too.

In a few minutes water was filling the hole and Katie sat back in disgust. "It's no use. We'll have to come back again at low tide."

Lorie hesitated a moment and then started digging again. "Anyway, we can build a sand castle," she said, heaping handfuls of wet sand in a pile and then dribbling sandy water over it to make fancy towers and balconies.

Katie started her own sand castle, building fast and furiously to catch up with Lorie. She jumped aside when a wave broke just on the other side of the driftwood and sent a sheet of water gliding in fast along the sand toward their castles.

"Quick! We've got to build a sea wall!" she cried. Then she sat back, staring at Lorie.

"What we've got to do is get back to the picnic," Lorie said.

They were scrambling up from the sand when they saw Katie's father jogging toward them, red-faced and panting.

"We were just coming," Katie called.

"And you'd better come in a hurry," he yelled and, turning around, started north again in a fast walk.

44

Katie and Lorie followed close at his heels. They were both tired, but they didn't complain. They had an idea that now was the time for silence, and for speed.

Katie wondered why her father hadn't brought the car. Then in a little while she saw for herself. He had had to leave it on the other side of the fallen palm tree. The tree was too big for him to drive over, he couldn't pass it on the root end because the water was too deep now, and the sand at the other end was so soft and deep he would have gotten stuck there for sure.

Still not talking, they got in the car and he tried to turn around. There was almost no hard beach now and the waves were washing over that. He had to back into the water and then pull up into the dry sand. Katie could feel the wheels sinking and hear the motor working hard, but her father eased his foot down on the gas pedal and the car pulled slowly forward. He finished the turn and they drove rapidly back down the beach.

Katie wasn't worried. Her daddy was a good driver and he was used to the beach. "Well!" she exclaimed. "That was almost an adventure."

He threw a worried look over his shoulder and then turned back to the beach. "We're not out of it yet, young lady."

They passed the spot where they'd had the picnic.

"Where's Mamma and Grandmother?"

"Up in the parking area by now. I hope."

When they got to the approach to the parking lot, the tide had covered the hard sand and they were running in shallow water. To get up to the safety of the pavement they would have to drive through deep ruts in very soft sand.

Her father gunned the motor. He needed good speed to drive through the ruts without getting stuck.

He didn't make it. His wheels spun around, sending the sand flying. He stopped, backed up, and tried again. This time was worse. The wheels ground deep down into the sand and the car slowed to a stop.

Katie's mother came running down from the parking lot. "Don't spin your wheels! You'll make it worse."

He glared at her, angry and helpless. "I know that, Kathryn. Don't you think I know that?"

He got out of the car and walked around it, looking down at the wheels and then at the water bubbling in along the soft sand. "It's no use," he said. "I'm really stuck! I can't get out of here without a tow truck. You take the girls on to town and send one out here."

Katie's mother looked at the moving water behind them and the soft sand at their feet. "At least the tide probably won't reach the car. It hasn't come this high for several days."

"Well, that's a comfort—a small one, but a comfort," he said crossly. He opened the door for Katie and Lorie to get out.

Katie slid by him and said with a small voice, "I'm sorry, Daddy."

He didn't even answer her.

• • ● • •

The next afternoon after her father had eaten a big Sunday dinner and was relaxing with his paper, Katie decided to try for another apology.

Last night on the way home her mother and grandmother had let her have it for going so far down the beach after she'd been told specifically not to.

"It didn't seem far when we were walking," Katie said. "Did it, Lorie? We didn't think about it being far."

Her grandmother shook her head. "No, because you had your mind set on one thing—looking for treasure. You just completely forgot your promise to me."

Her mother chimed in again. "You had no business being way down there all by yourselves anyway, and you could see the tide coming in. Where was your common sense?"

Katie sighed. "I said I was sorry. And Daddy's going to kill me anyway, so you don't have to keep fussing at me."

"Well, he won't do that, but after he pays for the tow truck he may cut off your allowance for about a million years."

Now Katie stood close to her father's chair thinking about what to say. She hated for him to be angry with her and she was worried about losing her allowance for what might be a very long time.

"I really am sorry, Dad," she said after a moment. "Did you notice I got up and got ready for Sunday school this morning without being called twice, and that I really listened to the sermon in church? I understood what Dr. Rice was saying, because Lorie and I had an argument about it last week. He said it is important to work for the Lord wherever we are and not to keep saying that someday we're going to do something for Him or be somebody important for Him. The

47

thing is, all God's work is important and all His workers are important, and if we aren't working for Him now, with the people around us, chances are we won't work for Him later either." She paused, thinking that what she was going to ask might not be her business. "Dad, I was wondering about Uncle Frank. Why doesn't he go to church?"

He looked up at her, shaking his head. "There isn't any real reason or excuse for his not going that I know of. He got out of the habit when he went off to school and then to Vietnam, and he's never gotten started back again."

"Well, I wish he'd go with us sometimes."

"I do too, Katie. Maybe you can help me work on him. I haven't been too successful up to this point."

"I'll help you, Daddy, and not just because of what Dr. Rice said this morning."

He caught her hand. "Honey, you remind me of the little girl in the nursery rhyme. When you're good you're very, very good, but when you're bad, you're horrid. You were pretty bad yesterday."

Katie looked down at her feet. "I didn't mean to do anything wrong. I was just having a lot of fun and I didn't think about the tide."

He sighed. "Well, okay. I believe you when you say you weren't deliberately disobedient and I hope you've learned a lesson. When we tell you not to do something, there's a reason for it. We're not just trying to cut you out of some fun."

He relaxed his face then and smiled at her. Katie smiled back. "Can I get you something Daddy? A cup of coffee? A coke?"

"No, no thanks." He picked up his paper again.

She didn't stir and he looked up at her. "Well, what else is on your mind?"

She started speaking slowly, and then finished in a rush. "Could you punish me in some other way besides taking my allowance? I've decided to save up to buy a metal detector, you know, so I can find treasure."

His smile disappeared and he shook his head. "Katie B. Reise! I wouldn't let you buy a metal detector, even if you had the money. You're too young to handle a thing like that and no telling what you'd get into if you could handle it. Now would you please let me read my paper?"

• • ● • •

Katie went out and sat on the back step of the patio, looking across the yard. This was such a dumb yard, plain old grass, neatly cut, shrubs in an even row and, in the corner, her grandmother's prize rose garden. Dull, dull—like her whole life.

Katie was sulking, and she knew she was sulking, but she didn't plan to stop anytime soon.

Her father wasn't being fair. She'd told him she was sorry and he'd said he forgave her. Then he'd turned right around and refused to even talk about her getting a metal detector. That was almost the same as saying she couldn't search for treasure. Katie began to sniffle down in the bend of her elbow. If her grandmother Reise were still alive she would understand that Katie had to keep searching for treasure.

Katie stopped sniffling and stared out in the yard. And if the grownups wouldn't help her, she'd just have to do it by herself, that's all there was to it.

49

3 • Lost in the Woods

Mrs. Bailey announced in Sunday school, "We'll have a picnic at the old fort on Saturday afternoon. We can celebrate the approaching end of another school year. You can explore and play games an hour or so, and then we'll cook hot dogs at the picnic grounds."

Katie wasn't too excited. She'd been to the old fort many times. Leaning over, she whispered to Lorie, "I'd rather go somewhere where there's lots of great things to do."

"There's lots to do at the fort, and you know it," Lorie whispered back. "You just always think something else is better than what you've already got."

Katie shrugged, knowing that Lorie was right, about the fort anyway. The fort was at the northern end of the island where the river joined the ocean. It was pentagon shaped, with brick buildings called bastions at each of its five corner. The bastions were also pentagon shaped, but Katie thought they really looked like ships with their bows pointed out to sea.

The corner buildings were joined by high, wide,

brick walls called ramparts. The moat dug around the outside of the walls used to have water in it. Even though it was usually dry now, Katie always pictured it full of water and alligators.

She loved to run along the tops of the ramparts from one corner to the next, and to climb down the narrow circular stairs into the bastions where there were storerooms to explore, more gun emplacements, and narrow slits in the walls where she could stand, pretending to spy out the enemy.

"Katie, would you like to be in charge of planning the games?" Mrs. Bailey asked.

"Uh, uh, well, why don't you ask Lisa?" Katie stammered. "She's really good at things like that."

Lorie stared at Katie, and Katie knew why. Katie always wanted to plan the games.

She stared back without a word. She had the beginning of a plan cooking in her mind, but it didn't include the class at all.

• • ● • •

On Saturday afternoon Katie and Lorie were the first ones out of the cars when they pulled into the fort's parking area. Katie caught Lorie's arm and rushed her along toward the gate. She hadn't told Lorie anything except that she had a really great idea for the two of them. She didn't want Lorie to have time to back out, or to tell anybody else the plan.

They ran across the bridge ahead of the others and through the arched brick tunnel leading to the parade grounds at the center of the fort.

Mrs. Bailey called out to them, "Katie! Lorie! Let's all stay together now."

"Oh, we're just going to race to see who can be first to the top of the wall," Katie answered, yanking on Lorie's arm.

"Take it easy, will you?" Lorie said. "We're supposed to tour the old jail, and the bakery, and all those buildings first."

"We've seen all that stuff a zillion times. Come on, I'll beat you up that ramp."

Both girls were good runners. They flew across the wide parade grounds and only slowed a little on the concrete ramp leading up to the top of one of the bastions jutting out to sea.

It was a near tie. "I would have won but my shoelace was untied," Katie said.

They panted a moment, breathing the stiff ocean breeze in gulps. Katie leaned on one hand against a corroded metal pole reaching high above their heads. It curved out over the ground below and had a hole at the end.

Katie tried to circle the pole with her hands. "I wish I knew how many bloodthirsty old pirates hung from this pole," she said.

"None, you dum-dum. This fort wasn't built until just before the Civil War. The pirates were gone before then. Besides, it's not a hanging pole. It's some kind of a pulley to lift things with."

Katie spoke with exasperation. "Do you have to ruin everything? You sound like my grandmother Bradbury." She turned to face the water. "When I'm on this wall I see pirate ships coming into the river down there on their way to the docks at the old settlement. I see their flags flying and the pirates swarming up the rigging, adjusting their sails to the winds." She looked at Lorie defiantly. "And that did happen."

Lorie shrugged.

"And I see one ship anchoring off the shore there on the beach before he got to the settlement. I see a longboat pulling out from the ship with pirates in it and old Blackbeard in the bow with his foot on a chest."

Lorie caught Katie's arm and the two girls stared out at the shining blue river running toward town away from the fort.

In a moment Katie turned and pointed dramatically to the oak woods behind the fort. "And that's where he went with the men and the treasure." She looked back toward the parade grounds where the other girls were running in and out of the old barracks with Mrs. Bailey trudging behind them. Then she leaned close to Lorie, "And that's where we're going."

This broke the spell for Lorie. "You're really crazy, you know that? Mrs. Bailey wouldn't let us go if we wanted to, and I don't want to anyway."

"Of course you want to. You want to find the treasure, don't you? And we're not going to ask Mrs. Bailey, we're just going. That way we won't be disobeying." Katie knew better, but she wanted to go more than she wanted to obey. And if they got back before Mrs. Bailey missed them, what was the harm?

Lorie groaned. "I'd rather stay here and eat our hot dogs."

"We'll be back for the hot dogs. See? We can slip out the broken place in the bricks down at the foot of this bastion. The guards are over toward the main gate and won't see us. Then we can scoot up into the woods and take a quick look around. We might spot the tree with the chain right off. Who knows? Then one of us can come back here for Mrs. Bailey." She paused. "I've decided not to be selfish. I'm going to split the treasure with the church. That's the same as giving it to God."

Katie gave Lorie a yank and they were off. Down the narrow spiraling stairway into the large room below, past the crack in the floor which Katie usually peered into, certain there was treasure or old bones in the darkness beneath the floor. She slipped through the broken wall, Lorie behind her, out into the bright sunlight on the white beach.

After the cool dampness of the fort, the sun was warm and pleasant. Several men were out on a small rock jetty fishing and Katie whispered, "Act normal. We don't want anyone to get suspicious. I don't mind sharing the treasure with God, but I have to draw the line somewhere."

They began walking around the edge of the fort to get to the inland side. It wasn't exactly a short walk.

"Are you sure we can get back for the hot dogs?" Lorie asked.

"If we find the treasure, you won't care about the hot dogs."

Scrubby trees and palmetto bushes grew close to the fort on the inland side. Katie and Lorie slipped across a narrow open space and were almost immediately swallowed up in a patch of trees thickly hung with moss and grape vines. They parted the underbrush with their hands, and stepped as tall as they could over the lowest branches growing in their way.

"There's probably a million rattlesnakes in here," Katie said, a little nervous for the first time. She paused for a moment, thinking about the snakes. The sweat was rolling down her face, and her shirt and jeans were filled with sandspurs and beggar lice. After just that moment she plunged on. When would they ever get another chance like this?

After a few minutes she stopped again, this time to get her bearings. She looked back across the way they'd come. "I figure Blackbeard came in from the river about there, and then cut straight across here and into the deep woods. Let's go!"

"Katie! How'll we ever get out again?"

"Trust me. I have a great sense of direction."

In among the trees there was deep shade, but because they were cut off from the breeze, it was much hotter than it had been out in the open. "This looks pretty piraty," Katie said, wiping off her face with her sleeve. "I think we can start looking now. Report immediately if you see anything suspicious."

They began checking out the trees from top to bottom, their moss-hung branches, their crooked, spindly trunks, their roots under the tangles of vines.

After examining several trees, Lorie said, "This is silly, Katie. The chain has got to be rusted away by now."

"But the bark would have a scar on it at least."

"After all these years?"

"Of course," Katie said authoritatively. Then she laughed. "Of course, there's always the ghost. He might show up and give us a clue." She paused a moment. Suddenly this didn't seem very funny. The

56

woods were pretty dark. Was it because the trees were thicker, or had they been gone longer than she'd planned?

"What time is it?" she asked.

"It's four-thirty," Lorie said with relief. "We have to start back because we're eating at five."

Katie couldn't give up this soon. "Just a couple more trees first," she said, skirting around a palmetto bush toward a tall pine.

"Well, this is as far as I'm going," Lorie said stubbornly. "It's getting late and I'm hungry."

Katie gave a sigh of exasperation. "Oh, all right, but you'll never find treasure if you give up so easy."

She came back to where Lorie was standing. Though she wouldn't admit it, she was ready to stop looking herself. She just hadn't realized what a job it would be to find one special tree once you were in the deep woods.

She looked around. Right now all the trees looked exactly alike. The underbrush was like a thick mat nobody had ever walked through.

Lorie was looking around too. "Which way is out?"

"Don't worry. All we have to do is head back towards the river. Then we can walk along the beach to the fort."

"Yeah, but which way is the river?"

Katie stood straight and looked at the thick trees surrounding them. Then she licked her finger and held it up. In a moment she said, "The breeze is coming from over that way. I think that must be the river."

"You think?" she repeated. "How about your great sense of direction?"

Katie shrugged, pretending a calm she didn't feel.

"You could climb a tree and look," Lorie suggested.

"Good idea, not that I needed it," Katie said and immediately started up an old cedar with branches low enough for her to climb on.

It was no use. She couldn't see a thing except branches and moss and a little sky. Coming down, she said, "Don't worry, we'll just follow the breeze. It's bound to be coming from the river."

They followed what was really a very small and not too steady breeze. They were hot and perspiring, their hands and faces scratched from thorny bushes, and their clothes thick with every kind of sticker. It was close to five now and the gnats and mosquitoes were beginning to bother them.

"This treasure hunt is the dumbest idea you ever had," Lorie complained. "And I'm super dumb for letting you talk me into coming."

"Hush up, will you? I'm trying to get us out of here."

Suddenly they burst into a small clearing bordering a stagnant pond. Katie knew they hadn't passed it coming in. "Great!" she said. "All we need is alligators."

Lorie grabbed her. "Katie! There aren't really any alligators here, are there?"

"Of course not. But we're getting away from here right now anyhow."

They turned and pushed back into the bushes.

After just a few minutes Lorie said, "Stop, Katie. Stop right now. Don't go any further. We're lost. We're lost in this horrible woods and you know it."

Katie stopped and looked back at her friend. Until Lorie had said the word *lost*, Katie hadn't allowed herself to think it. She thought it now and she was afraid, but she wasn't going to let Lorie know that.

"We should stop and think what's the best thing to do," she said. What was the best thing to do? She didn't even know. They could wait in one place hoping a ranger or a hiker would come through. But it was getting toward dark. Nobody would be coming this way this time of day. There was just one hope and she expressed it.

"Mrs. Bailey has missed us by now. She'll send a ranger in looking for us. He's probably already looking. All we have to do is stay put and maybe holler for help every so often."

"Help, help!" Lorie yelled immediately.

"Help, help! We're over here!" Katie shouted.

They got quiet then and listened, but the only sound was from the birds and the insects in the trees and bushes.

"We'll wait a few minutes and yell again," Katie said. "I'm not worried. They'll send word back to town and my uncle Frank will come find us. He knows these woods. Even my daddy will come if he knows we're lost."

"My daddy will come too and he'll kill me," Lorie groaned.

Katie began to shout again and then stopped suddenly. She'd just had a really terrible thought. There was somebody else in these woods who might find them first.

Petey Moon!

She grabbed Lorie's arm. "Look, we've got to be quiet and not mess around, but just walk out of here."

"How? How?"

"I don't know, but we've got to try." She took Lorie's hand. "For starters, why don't we pray? After all, we're on a Sunday school picnic, aren't we?"

"We *were* on a Sunday school picnic, Katie. God doesn't even know where we are now."

"He knows where we are. He knows where everybody is all the time. Now let's just pray while we keep walking."

Katie prayed harder than she had ever prayed before. She told God she was sorry she had run away from the picnic and if He'd just help them out of the woods she would never do such a dumb and bad thing again. Besides that, she was going to start paying attention to Mrs. Bailey, and she was going to cooperate with her grandmother a little better.

She hadn't prayed long until she saw what looked like a break in the woods ahead. Through the trees she thought she saw the outline of a house.

"Come on, come on!" she said, pulling hard at Lorie. "I told you it would help to pray."

It was a house. At least it had once been a house. It seemed to be held up only by hub caps and snake skins nailed to its sagging boards.

Katie stopped, staring. She knew without being told that this was Petey Moon's house.

Lorie bumped into Katie and then she saw the house. "We're saved! We can use their telephone!"

As frightened as she was, Katie looked at Lorie with disgust. "You've got to be kidding. A telephone in that shack? Besides, don't you know whose place that is?''

Lorie stared at Katie and then at the old house. "Petey Moon's house," she whispered. "We've found Petey Moon's house in the woods."

From somewhere very close by a heavy voice spoke. "Somebody lookin' for old Petey Moon?"

They heard the voice but they couldn't see who had spoken. Nothing moved around the old shack, not even a skinny dog. They hadn't heard a footstep or even a twig breaking.

Katie held tight to Lorie's hand, wanting to run but not knowing which way to go.

"Whut you chillun doin' out heah in Petey Moon's woods?"

A figure materialized in the trees beside them. If they'd been watching a TV show Katie would have thought he'd been beamed down from a space ship. But the man staring at them was no creature from outer space.

He was tall and wide, with long shaggy hair and black eyes. He had on old army pants, a black suit jacket, and a ragged knit cap. Over his shoulder was a canvas bag full of heaven knew what.

It was Petey Moon all right. Katie had seen him at a distance lots of times and nobody else looked like that.

"Oh, God," she groaned inside. "You're not helping us."

He moved closer to them.

"We were just leaving," Katie said and shoved Lorie to get her going.

In one giant step he was beside them. Reaching out, he grabbed each of them by an arm. "Don't go tearin' off in them woods no moah. It's neah about dark. The gators gonna get you."

"No, they won't," Lorie said, trying to pull away. "Our fathers are waiting for us just over there in the woods."

"Maybe so, maybe not," he said, but he didn't let them go.

He pushed them ahead of him through the small clearing to his house. Unlatching the door he shoved them inside and over toward a broken-down old couch. "Sit down theah," he said, and they did.

He stopped for a moment as if he was thinking. Then he dropped the bolt in a lock on the door too high for them to reach.

Katie would have started screaming, but she had a strange and comforting feeling. This was just another of her bad dreams. In a minute she would wake up in her room and old Lady Jane would be by her on her bed. In this dream she'd have to make do with Lorie. She moved a little closer to her on the couch.

Lorie moved away and looked at her with wide-open accusing eyes. "Now s-s-see what you've gotten us into," she stuttered.

This made Katie so angry she didn't tell Lorie she was only part of a dream. Katie looked around the shadowy room. On one wall was a fireplace with a mantle over it made from half a log. Animal skins were stretched out on all the walls, and over the fireplace was a rattlesnake skin about ten feet long.

Petey Moon was lighting a kerosene lamp, the kind her father kept in case of a hurricane. It made the room seem spookier. Then he moved, a giant-sized spook himself, over to a pump in the rusty sink hanging crooked off the wall. The pump made a dry, scraping sound when he worked the handle and no water came out. He picked up a pan from the sink and poured some water in the top of the pump.

Katie whispered, "While he's busy we've got to escape." But how? They couldn't get out the door without dragging a chair over to it, and the windows had boards nailed across their bottom halves.

Petey Moon was still working at the pump, his back to them. In just a minute water began pouring from the mouth of the pump. He filled two thick mugs and brought them to the girls.

Katie stared at the grimy mug he was handing her, and then at him. Was this like the last meal before the electric chair? Poison maybe? Or was it just plain water? He scowled so fiercely at her hesitation that she took a cup and nudged Lorie to do the same.

It was plain water, at least it was plain sulphur water, the kind you got at the beach. And it was cold. It would have been great really, if she hadn't been so frightened.

Petey Moon went to one of the windows and stood looking out for what seemed like a long time. Then he turned and came back to them. The girls leaned hard on each other.

"We go now," he said.

"Wh-where?" Katie stammered.

He didn't answer but strode to the door and lifted the bolt. Any thought Katie had of making a wild run for freedom was cut off when he grabbed her arm and then Lorie's. He pulled them out the door and started dragging them through the clearing which by now was pretty dark.

When the first briar branch at the edge of the woods whipped across her face Katie began to cry softly. She knew this wasn't a dream. She had gotten herself and Lorie in a real mess. She didn't see any way at all of getting them out. It didn't look as if the Lord was going to help either.

She stopped pulling against Petey Moon and walked along as best she could, following what seemed to be some sort of path.

It wasn't long before she heard a new kind of noise. At first she was afraid to trust her ears. Then she had to trust them for she was unmistakably hearing the sound of cars going by on a paved road. Soon she could see lights flashing through the trees.

She looked over at Lorie to see if she was seeing and hearing the same thing. They nodded at each other, with excitement and hope. Petey Moon yanked them through the last of the trees and they were on the grassy right of way beside a wide road.

Katie recognized it at once. The beach road! The good old beach road that led into town.

She tried to break away from Petey Moon, but he held her in an iron grip. Then he pulled them back a little way into the trees. "You wait," he demanded.

They waited. Several cars passed. Katie waved with her free hand. Then she yelled, "Stop, stop!"

Petey Moon jerked her back. "I say you wait."

And so they waited and nobody stopped. The cars were going too fast for the drivers to see three people standing in the near dark.

This waiting was the worst time of all. Safety was so near!

Then in the distance Katie saw a white car coming with a lighted bar across its top. A police car!

In just that second Petey Moon released them. "Now you go," he said.

Katie grabbed Lorie and they scrambled to the edge of the road waving their arms and yelling, "Help, police, help!"

Brakes screeched and the police car stopped just on the other side of them and then pulled off the road. Two police jumped out and the girls ran to them and collapsed in their arms.

"We've been lost in the woods," Lorie cried.

"And Petey Moon found us!" Katie added.

One of the policemen spoke to the other. "Pick him up. Maybe we've finally got something on the old devil."

Katie grabbed his arm. "No, no. He didn't do anything bad. He was helping us all the time and we didn't even know it."

The policemen looked a little disappointed. Katie had another thought. They hadn't thanked the scary old man. She wheeled around and looked down the road to where they'd been waiting. She knew now they had been waiting for a car Petey Moon was sure they'd be safe in.

The roadside was dark and empty. Petey Moon had vanished into the woods.

• • ● • •

Katie could hear the grownups talking in the family room down the hall. She was glad to hear them talk because up to now nobody had said much to her or to each other. Her mother had helped her get the stickers out of her hair before shampooing it, and she stood by while Katie scrubbed her whole body with hot water and soap to get the chiggers off. Then she'd brought her a tray with a sandwich and some milk.

"You know you're in a lot of trouble?" she'd asked.

"Yes, ma'am."

"I'm grateful to the Lord that Petey Moon found you and helped you get home safely. I certainly misjudged the old man and I'm sorry for that. But what is troubling me now is that you seem to have gone from bad to worse in this treasure hunting thing. On the beach the other day I think you were just careless when you went too far away, but today you had to know it was wrong to leave the group and go off into the woods."

Katie nodded. "I knew it was wrong, but I wanted to go so bad and I didn't think anybody would ever take me."

"Just wanting to do something doesn't give you a license to do it, Katie. You're going to find a lot of things in life you want to do. But as a Christian you have to ask yourself if God would want you to do them, or if your doing them will hurt you or anybody else.

"In this case you went off without permission, and you dragged Lorie along with you. I'm not excusing her, but you certainly have been a bad influence on her. And together you scared poor Mrs. Bailey half to death."

"I was scared too, Mamma. More than ever in my life."

"I'm sure you were." Her mother sighed. "I think you need to make some apologies, first to God and then to some other people you've upset today."

"Yes, ma'am. Mamma, will you stay and hear my prayers like when I was little?"

"Of course, dear." Katie's mother sat down by her on the bed and she and Katie bowed their heads.

"Dear God, I'm sorry for what I did. I'm sorry I upset Mrs. Bailey and my family. Please forgive me and help me not to be so mule-headed. And when I look for treasure again," she stole a peek at her mother who had her eyes shut tight, "help me to do it in a right way. Amen."

"Amen," her mother said, and leaned over to kiss her. "Go to sleep. We'll talk some more tomorrow."

Now the grownups were talking themselves. Katie couldn't hear what they were saying, but she had a pretty good idea who they were saying it about.

• • ● • •

"You can't just ignore a thing like this," Katie's grandmother said.

"I know that," Katie's mother answered. "But I think she's already had a great deal of punishment. She was really quite frightened."

"I'm not talking about punishment. I'm talking about some kind of discipline to help her learn something from this experience. She needs time to really think about it."

"Yeah, but you don't want to curb that great spirit of adventure she has," Frank said.

Katie's father spoke up. "Well, that great spirit has

got to be brought under control. She has to accept realistically that she's still young and can't go charging off alone in all directions whenever the notion strikes her."

"Why don't you take her some of the places she wants to go?" Katie's mother asked.

"Sorry, I'm not a treasure hunter. And I don't have time."

"I'll take her," Frank said. "We can go out by the old Indian campground and dig around there. We won't likely find treasure, but it'll be an interesting place for her to explore."

Mrs. Bradbury shook her head. "I don't mean to be negative here, but shouldn't that be saved as a sort of reward when her conduct improves?"

There was a little silence and then Katie's mother said, "Mamma's right. We'll just have to hold that for a while, Frank. I guess we ought to ground her for at least two weeks."

"With no television and no company," Katie's father added. "That will give her time to make up her mind not to pull any more wild stunts like this one this afternoon."

"And of course, she must go and apolozie to Mrs. Bailey right away," Katie's mother said. "That poor lady is threatening to resign."

• • ● • •

Katie went by herself to Mrs. Bailey's house on Sunday afternoon. She had hoped her mother would go with her, or at least Lorie, but her parents said this was something that she needed to do alone.

Lorie couldn't have gone anyway because her parents had taken her off to visit cousins in Georgia. Katie suspected they wanted to get Lorie away from her for a few hours.

Mrs. Bailey was expecting her. She was sitting out on her big screened porch with all her hanging baskets. She even had lemonade and thin sugar cookies waiting, with two plates and two glasses, which made Katie feel guilty.

"Sit down and have some lemonade, Katie. You must be hot and tired." She didn't call her "Precious." Katie guessed that would have been expecting too much.

"Yes, ma'am, but first I have to say I'm sorry I ran away from the picnic and upset you." Katie took a deep breath and went on. "And I hope you won't resign as our teacher. You tell us a lot of good things which from now on I'm going to try to remember." Katie hadn't planned to say that last part, but with the lemonade and all it only seemed fair. Besides, that's what she'd promised God if He helped her get out of the woods!

"Well, that's very sweet of you, Katie. I know I seem old-fashioned to you girls, but I do love you. And I want very much to teach those things about God which will always be true no matter who's teaching or who's listening."

"Yes, ma'am, I know."

"I told your grandmother when she called that I had decided not to resign."

"My grandmother called?"

"Yes, she did. She said she would like to work with

me in Sunday school in the Girls' Mission Club. She said she knew she needed to get involved with the work of the church here, and this seemed a good place to start."

Katie gulped. Mrs. Bailey and her grandmother at the same time!

"But I told her I had prayed about it and decided that it isn't right to quit a job that you think is important just because you're upset. Maybe I need to be more flexible with you girls at some points. I did suggest that your grandmother help with the high school group. Those girls have been needing a leader for a long time."

Mrs. Bailey poured Katie a tall glass of lemonade and put it on a plate with some cookies. "Don't you think that would be a good idea?"

"Super," Katie said.

• • ● • •

At school the next Monday, Lorie and Katie sat on a bench eating their lunches in near silence.

Lorie had just told Katie that as big as she was she had gotten a hard spanking Saturday night. "It was humiliating," she sniffed.

Katie dropped a crust of bread on the ground for the ants and said in disgust, "I'd rather get spanked and get it over with than be stuck in the house for two weeks."

"Can you watch TV?"

"No. I have to work on some kind of useful project with my grandmother. Can you believe that?" She scuffed the sand with her tennis shoes. "I guess I deserve it though." She looked up at Lorie. "Anyway, if I

70

behave myself, later on Uncle Frank's going to take me to the Indian campground to dig. You want to go with us?"

Lorie folded her sandwich bag, put it in her lunch box, and snapped the lid shut. "No, thank you. I don't want to see any more woods of any kind for a while."

"Well, I do. This is a whole new place to look and you don't know what I might find."

"Not a treasure, I bet."

Katie glared at her. "Oh, you don't think so? Well, maybe without you tagging along, slowing me down, I'll have a lot better chance at finding one!"

Lorie didn't answer. She just looked at Katie as if her feelings were hurt. Then, getting up, she started back toward the school.

Katie shrugged. There wasn't any reason for Lorie to act so touchy. Weren't they always jawing at each other without taking it seriously?

Katie walked toward school by herself. She started to call out to Lorie to wait up, but then she didn't. If Lorie wanted to get angry and stay angry for no reason at all, then let her. Katie had other things to think about besides Lorie.

4 · Useful Projects

When Katie's grandmother suggested the first useful project it sounded pretty grim.

"We're going to give your room a total clean-up job," she said.

"Ohhhh, Grandmother!" Katie groaned.

"It hasn't been done in a long time, certainly not since I've been here. What I want you to do is to empty out your closet, your dresser drawers, and your shelves. I'll get boxes from the store for you to put the real junk in, and to set aside the good things you're ready to give away. Then it won't be hard for you to neatly organize the rest."

"That'll take years!"

"Not really, but it will take several days. I'll be glad to help you any way I can. There's nothing I'd rather do than tackle a job like this. It's so satisfying to get things really organized."

At that moment Katie thought she would never learn to like her grandmother. Unless of course she was just kidding. But she wasn't.

"I suggest you hop to it as soon as you've had your snack, Katie," she said. "Get a good start on it before supper."

• • ● • •

By suppertime Katie was beginning to realize that she had more stuff stashed away than anybody ought to keep in one room. There were parts and pieces of games, craft sets half completed, books everywhere except on the book shelves, and stuffed animals in every condition from impossible to nearly new.

The biggest problem was her dolls. Although it had been a long time since she'd actually played with any of them, she had kept almost every one she'd ever owned. There was a soft rag doll with a flat, smooth face; a baby doll that ate and wet its pants; a Shirley Temple that had belonged to her mother; Barbie dolls; European dolls with stiff dresses in bright colors and much lace; and an Indian pair in leather dresses. And of course, Lady Jane, the last doll her other grandmother had given her.

Besides the dolls, there were two cardboard boxes full of all kinds of tiny dresses and blankets and all sorts of doll-sized accessories.

Katie piled everything in the doll category on her bed and then sat down in a chair wondering what she was going to do with it all.

Her grandmother came in just then. "Well, you've made a real good start in pulling stuff out." She put a stack of boxes down by Katie's bed. "Why don't you cull out what you consider trash first and get that out of your way. Then you can start separating the good stuff you want to give away. We can put that in the garage." She looked at the bed full of dolls. "Any of these you want to give away?"

Katie frowned. "I don't think so, but I'm going to put them away, most of them anyhow. I may keep out a couple of the prettiest ones for decoration, and of course, Lady Jane stays on my bed."

"Of course," her grandmother said. "Had you thought of washing up all the clothes and dolls that can be washed, and redressing the dolls before putting them away?"

"No, but I could," Katie said, scowling. "I've got plenty of time."

"You know, by the time you're grown up some of your dolls will probably be collector's items. Your mother's Shirley Temple is one now and you should take especially good care of her. If I still had my Bye-Lo Baby from when I was a little girl she would be quite valuable. But I made the mistake of trying to take her for a ride on my tricycle and her dear china head was smashed to smithereens."

"Ohhh," Katie said. "Did you cry?"

"Yes, I did. A long time."

"I would have too. You know, if I was little enough to ride a tricycle."

"Of course." Grandmother picked up the soft and floppy rag doll with the pink smile painted on her sleepy face. "I like old Sleepy here. She's got real personality."

She looked at Katie. "You know, I've just had what might be a good idea. Remember the old-fashioned china cabinet out in the garage that your father brought from your other grandmother's house? It could be cleaned up, maybe even refinished. It would make a wonderful display cabinet for your dolls."

The idea interested Katie. "But would he let me have it just for dolls?"

"We can always ask. And if he agrees we'll get to work cleaning it up so that it'll look nice with your furniture." She paused and looked around at the piles of stuff all over the room and on Katie's bed. "But first, we have to excavate your furniture!"

• • ● • •

It was almost the end of the second week before Katie's room was finished. She and her grandmother had ended up refinishing the cabinet. Fortunately it only had the original coat of varnish on it. Katie's grandmother explained that some old pieces like this had six or seven coats of paint on them, one on top of the other, which made them really hard to clean.

Her father and uncle Frank carried the cabinet out in the side yard next to the garage, and put it on a sheet covered with old newspapers.

"If I weren't so busy at the store, I'd do this myself," her father said. "And you guys be careful. I always liked this old cabinet."

Katie had never paid any attention to the cabinet, but now that she was going to use it in her room she was a lot more interested.

It had been built of what her grandmother called golden oak. It had a curved front made of panels of glass framed with strips of wood. The two front panels opened out to make the door and could be fastened shut again with a fancy little brass lock and key. There were five shelves to hold her dolls.

76

After cleaning all the dust and dirt off the cabinet they put on rubber gloves and began painting it section by section with thick coats of paint remover. In about twenty minutes the varnish would get soft and gooey and they could begin to scrape it off with their flat scraping tools. Katie's grandmother did the hard part next to the glass and showed Katie how to scrape carefully so as not to dig into the wood.

Some places on the cabinet had to have a second coat of the remover. During the process of getting it thoroughly clean both Katie and her grandmother got pretty sweaty and dirty, with smudges of varnish on their arms and faces.

Katie had never seen her grandmother actually dirty, and found this new picture rather impressive.

On the afternoon they finally finished, her grandmother looked down at herself and made a face. "What a mess," she said, "but it was worth it. I think we did a good job. And you were very patient, Katie. I'm proud of you."

Katie shrugged, not quite willing to admit she'd had fun working on the cabinet.

"Now let's get rid of all these newspapers and other trash while we're still dirty ourselves, and tomorrow we can put the finishing touches on the cabinet." She stood back and looked at it. "I think we'll just rub it down with a tung oil mixture as a finish. I like the natural look, don't you?"

Katie put her hands on her hips and studied the cabinet carefully. She hadn't the slightest idea of what a good finish would be, but she liked the sound of the word natural. "Yes, let's do it that way. Gran'ma Reise was a natural person and after all, this was her cabinet."

Her grandmother nodded. "Yes, you're right, Katie, and natural it will be."

• • ● • •

The softly shining cabinet looked great in Katie's room, especially when she'd filled it with her dolls.

She clapped her hands excitedly. "I've got to call Lorie to come over and see it." She started for the telephone and then stopped. "I forgot. My two weeks aren't up yet."

Her mother, who had just walked in, answered. "That's right, Katie. Lorie will have to wait till next week to see the transformation. We've got two school afternoons and the weekend left. That's time enough to do a second project."

Katie felt let down and looked at her grandmother suspiciously. "I guess you've already thought of one."

"Well, as a matter of fact I have. With your parents' permission we're going to move from here to the library."

Katie's eyes opened wide. "We're going to reorganize the library?"

Her grandmother laughed. "No. But we're going to get some books for a research project."

"Research project?"

"Yes. And on your favorite subject. Buried treasure. We're going to see if we can find out if there really is any buried treasure around here, and what, if anything, you can do as a young girl to look for it."

Katie clapped her hands together and her mother laughed. "That doesn't sound much like discipline."

78

Her grandmother said, "Well, you only said she had to work on useful projects. You didn't say they couldn't be fun."

• • ● • •

Katie was sitting at the kitchen table feeling a little grumpy when her father came in from work.

"Well, what's wrong with my one and only daughter?" he asked, pulling off his suit coat. "Didn't you find anything interesting or promising at the library?"

Katie sat up straight in her chair. "Daddy, there really is treasure in Florida. Buried treasure, and a lot of valuable stuff is out under the water, especially off the west coast of Florida. Grandma and I found out that years and years ago a whole fleet of Spanish galleons just loaded with treasure was shipwrecked over there during a hurricane. Salvage crews have brought up gold chains and dishes and coins and all kinds of neat stuff. And there's plenty still there waiting under the water for some lucky person to find." She sighed.

"You don't figure you're that lucky person?"

"How can I be? You have to have zillions of dollars for equipment to find it and bring it up, and licenses to hunt, and all that kind of complicated thing."

He shrugged. "Tough luck for kids."

She nodded. "My only chance at all is to find something buried around here in a place I'm *allowed* to go." She couldn't help scowling when she said that. "And, of course, I really need a metal detector to do that." She paused. "And you've said I can't even have that."

He nodded. "You know why. Not only is it expensive but I'm afraid that with a piece of equipment like that you'd get carried away and do something dumb or dangerous."

She started to protest but he waved her down. "I don't want to discuss it." He picked up a book lying on the kitchen table beside her. "What's this?"

"It's about something you don't want to discuss. It's a whole book about how to look for treasure on land, and it's especially about how to use a metal detector."

He looked at her.

"Well, I can read about it, can't I?" she asked. "I can't do anything dumb or dangerous just reading about it, can I?"

"With you, Katie, it might be possible." He shuffled through a few pages and read the captions under several pictures. "It does look pretty interesting. Go on and read all you want to. Sure beats watching those moronic shows on TV."

• • ● • •

Later that night, when Katie came out of her room to get a drink of milk before she went to bed, she glanced in the family room to say a final goodnight. Her father was too interested in the book he was reading to do more than glance up and smile.

What interested Katie was that he was reading her library book about looking for treasure.

5 • Real Indians Lived Here

The next Saturday Katie's uncle Frank came through on his promise to take Katie exploring in the woods down on the south end of the island. He tried to make it clear to her that they were not really looking for treasure. They were just going to check around the site of an old Indian village to see what they could see.

Katie didn't believe him. She was sure he really had some secret knowledge of a treasure and he was going to help her find it.

"How deep in the woods can we go?" she asked when she had climbed into the cab of his old pickup truck.

"As far as you want to go, within reason. A buddy of mine owns the property around the old site and we can explore all through there." He grinned. "You know, if we find anything really valuable, we'll have to share."

She nodded, certain now that he really did have some clue he hadn't told her about. "That would be only fair," she said.

They drove along the river road toward the end of

the island. At one point he stopped and pointed out over the river. "You see that buoy right beyond that cove in the marsh?"

She nodded.

"Well, somewhere close to that buoy there's a fresh-water spring that bubbles right up to the surface of the river. I've found it a few times when I was out fishing. In the old days ships used to sail in here to fill their water barrels."

Katie sat up straight and stared at the river. "Pirate ships?"

"All kinds of ships."

"Wow! If I had lived then I could have sat right here and watched them."

He laughed. "Katie B., you've watched more exciting things on TV than girls in that day ever even dreamed existed."

"I know," she said impatiently. "But that's not the same, and it doesn't make me *not* want to see pirate ships!"

He drove on then, turned down a sandy road, and pulled into a clearing at the edge of the woods. A narrow trail led off between the trees.

Her uncle pointed down the trail. "Back in the old days there were all kinds of Indian settlements on the island, several down here on the south end. The site we're going to explore is just down this trail, a nice little walk from either the ocean or the river, and close to a fresh-water lake. A pretty nice place to live, I'd say. There used to be Indian mounds all along here, but they've been plundered by treasure hunters, like you, or bulldozed down in some places for paleface house builders. All the same, I can take you to what's left of a large burial mound, and maybe you can spot some interesting relics left behind by other searchers."

Katie had been listening with excitement and impatience. "Let's go! Let's go!" she said, climbing out of the cab of the truck.

He pulled a small spade out of the back of the truck. "Just in case," he said, winking at Katie.

Then he started down the trail, pushing aside palmetto fronds and underbrush as he went. She followed close behind. Sometimes a branch flapped in her face, sometimes she ran into spider webs and even spiders. They were huge, with bright-colored bodies. She knew they were not the kind to hurt you, but they looked ferocious.

"Ugh, get away," she said once, stopping to shake her hair wildly and brush at her face and clothes.

"Are you still with me?" her uncle Frank called. "Or is this too wild for you?"

"Of course it isn't too wild," she said, hurrying to catch up with him. "After all, I've tramped Petey Moon's woods and that was much worse than this."

"Don't make comparisons yet. We're just getting started."

The trees began to get closer together and taller, the underbrush thicker. Katie stayed close behind her uncle Frank.

In just a little while he stopped, looking all around. "It should be about here." He moved between a couple more trees. "Here, here it is."

Katie was disappointed at what they had found. She didn't know what she had been expecting, but this was just a wide, caved-in space in the woods, with a slightly raised ring of earth circling it. Small trees were growing both in the sunken place and around the rim.

"This is an Indian mound?" she asked, walking over the rim and down into the shallow hole.

"What's left of it. It probably used to look a little like a hill, could have been ten or fifteen feet high. It had the bodies of Indians and a few of their possessions in it. Down through the years trophy hunters and just plain curious people have dug into it and scattered everything. The wind and rain have done the rest. It's a dirty shame."

Katie scuffed the rotted leaves at her feet. "Since it's already ruined, can I dig a little?"

"Sure, why not? There's nothing to protect anymore." He pointed to several trees outside the ruined mound with red cloths tied around their trunks. "The surveyors have been here recently. This whole place will be leveled soon."

Katie tried to dig first at the bottom and then into the raised rim at one side of the hole. There were so many roots and vines she couldn't make any headway.

Her uncle Frank took the shovel then, and dug for her wherever she pointed. She was feeling let down now. He certainly didn't act as if he knew where there was any treasure. The only thing he was producing from all his digging was a lot of sweat. In a moment she said, "That's okay. All the good things were probably taken away before I was even born."

He wiped his forehead against his sleeve. "Yeah, I know. You wish you had lived before those lucky guys got here."

She made a face at him and began scuffing at the leaves again. She was disappointed in her uncle. She'd thought he could come up with something special.

"Let's walk over a little toward the river," he said.

Just on the other side of a heavy patch of trees they came to a cleared place covered with bleached white shells.

"Looks like somebody had a humongous oyster roast," Katie said.

"Well, a lot of different oyster roasts. The Indians ate lots of oysters and other shellfish and this is where they threw their shells. I can remember when there were really tall heaps here, called middens. But various building companies have sent trucks in and hauled them off for roads and so forth."

Katie had gone to a lot of oyster roasts, and this place seemed a lot more real to her than the old mound had been. "Wow! Real Indians eating real oysters and clams right here!"

"They were here, all right. Guale and Timucua mostly. But they're all long gone now."

He put the spade over his shoulder. "Well, that's about all there is to see around here now. We'd better get on back." They started to walk through the trees, her uncle sometimes using the spade to push small bushes aside. Then he stopped and bent down to pick up something.

It was a very large sea shell. He brushed away the leaves and dirt, then showed it to her. "Look at this old whelk, Honey. It's perfect, not even chipped. It's the biggest one I've ever seen."

"Yeah," she said, taking it from him and emptying

the loose dirt out of its center. "I've never seen one this big either."

"You know, the Indians used to gouge out tree trunks with this kind of shell to make their canoes."

"But not with this one."

"No, it's too perfect to have been used as a tool. Take it home, Katie. You can wash and polish it, and it'll be a pretty thing to sit on your dresser."

Katie smiled and nodded, but she thought, Wait'll I show Lorie the *treasure* I found. She'll burst her sides laughing.

• • ● • •

Late that afternoon Katie's grandmother looked up from the bowl of fresh green beans she was breaking in small pieces and said to Katie, "I'm afraid you hurt your uncle Frank's feelings today."

"No, I didn't. How could I have done that?"

"Well, he gave up a whole morning to take you on a lovely tramp through the woods. He thought you would be thrilled to see the site of the old Indian settlement."

Katie thought a moment. "I was interested, Grandmother, but not what you would call thrilled. You've got to understand that what would be thrilling would be to find something really great. A treasure chest! Or even a measly old bag of coins. Something valuable like that."

Her grandmother looked over at the shell sitting on a newspaper in the middle of the kitchen table and then back at Katie. After a moment she said, "Katie, very few people ever find big treasures of gold like you're talking about. There just aren't that many to be found. But in God's beautiful world, anyone can find small treasures like this old, perfect shell. You must learn to recognize the small treasures when you do find them, and take joy in what you find."

Katie picked up the shell and wiped away a bit of molded leaf clinging to it. "I take joy in this shell, especially since Uncle Frank helped me find it."

Her grandmother nodded. "That's an important point. The whelk is beautiful in itself, but it's especially beautiful because your uncle helped you find it. And the way he cares about you is a whole other treasure, a genuinely valuable one."

Katie dusted at the shell with her fingers. "Well, I care about him too, a whole bunch." She took the shell to the sink then, and washed it carefully, getting all the sand out of the inside with a soft bottle brush. Then she put it out on the window ledge to dry.

When her father came in that night from work, she was polishing the shell with baby oil. She jumped up and waved it at him.

"Look at this beautiful old shell, Daddy. Uncle Frank found it for me. Could you maybe take me over to his house after supper to show him how pretty it turned out? And I want to invite him to our special Girls' Club program at church next month. Wouldn't that be an easy way for him to start coming back?"

• • ● • •

Katie was almost in heaven. Her father and uncle were sitting on her uncle's porch talking about the old times, when they were kids. Katie was sitting on the steps listening, not moving much except to wave away mosquitoes when they hummed around her face. She didn't interrupt the men, even when she had a good question. She didn't want to remind them that it might be her bedtime.

"The beach isn't so much fun anymore, now that the tourists have found it," her Uncle Frank said. "Remember when you could go down on the south end and never see another soul except some guy fishing? The only trash you saw was natural, like driftwood or crab shells washed up by the tide. Now we've got crowds, and cars driving too fast, and people throwing garbage all over the place."

Her father nodded. "The Bicentennial crowd in '76 was pretty decent. I think most people had a special feeling about that day and wanted to keep things in fair order. Katie, you remember that day. We closed off Center Street and put up booths for games and crafts and good things to eat. There were races down on the beach and that night the city shot off some really great fireworks."

"Of course, I remember it!" Katie cried, not able to stay out of the conversation any longer. She jumped up to go stand by her father. "I especially remember the guys dressed up like pirates. They went around wagging their beards and waving their swords and stealing kisses from the ladies." She sighed. "Actually, real pirates used to do a lot more exciting things than that around here."

"Yeah, the real guys stole treasure and buried it or each other," her father said, winking at her uncle Frank as if he didn't believe in pirates at all, much less here on this island.

88

She went back to sit on the steps, but after a moment she said, "There were pirates here, and they did bury treasure, but I'm never going to find any of it."

Her uncle got up, spread his arms out in a big stretch and then turned to Katie. "Well, I don't know about finding any pirate treasure, but I'm thinking we ought to do some serious looking for the treasure that's supposed to be buried right here in this yard. I can't help believing there's something to the old tale. I think we ought to get a metal detector and go over the whole yard."

Katie jumped up again and ran over to him. "Oh, Uncle Frank, that's what I truly want to do, but I can't. Daddy won't let me buy one because he says I'm too young."

"Yeah, and I can't buy one either right now because I'm broke," her uncle said, "but I could rent one. I may just have to do that one of these days."

Katie looked at him anxiously. One of these days could be one of these years or never.

"Couldn't you just do it right away, like next week, like Monday, maybe?"

The two men laughed and Katie's feelings were a little hurt. She looked down at her hands.

"Sorry, Miss Katie. It can't be Monday. I'm fixing to take off for a few weeks of fishing down around Mexico with my buddies. I can't go chasing ghosts any more with you right now."

At just that moment her father got up from his chair. "Well, Katie, I might just do some chasing around with you myself. You've got a birthday coming up next week. Maybe I'll rent the detector and we'll celebrate your birthday looking for treasure. How does that sound?"

Katie answered by hugging him furiously. Then she ran over and gave her uncle an equally fierce hug. "Thanks, Uncle Frank, for a super idea."

"You're my favorite gal," he said. "Now wish me luck on my fishing trip. I may not see you till I get back."

"If you get back in time, will you come to my Recognition Service at church? I've got a long Scripture part to say, and I'm going to wear a costume from some other country, and everything!"

"Whissst, pchew," he whistled through his teeth. "Sounds like a very important occasion. If I get back in time I'll have to try to get there."

"That'll be great, and I hope you catch a lot of fish and every day I'll pray for you to be safe on the water."

He looked at her father and then back at her with a little smile. "You do that, Katie. It takes a lot of praying to keep a fella like me safe."

6 • When the Detector Goes Beep

Katie's father rented the detector the day before her birthday. That way they could try it in the backyard and not waste time practicing the next morning.

He and Katie had agreed it was better to rent a fairly good one than to buy a cheap one. If she kept her interest in this project, she could keep saving money and some day could buy one for herself. He'd even brought her a catalogue showing a lot of different models to dream over in the meantime.

"This model is pretty simple," he said, trying to get it out of the car while Katie jumped up and down in his way. He rested it on the ground by the car. "See this metal box up here has these knobs to operate it. Then this long shaft goes down to this plastic thing at the bottom that's shaped like a plate. It's actually the housing for electronic coils that detect the metal under the ground. This particular detector will locate metal of all sizes and gives the same beep for anything it finds. The better ones give you clues about the size of what's under the ground. But even with that one you'd still have to practice and learn to read the clues."

"Well, come on, come on. Let's go practice with this one," Katie said, grabbing the handle and starting to push the plate along the grass.

"Don't you want to know how it works?"

"I know how it works. It sounds out a radio signal in a steady hum until something metal messes it up. Then it beeps really loud and you know you've found something."

"Humph. Well, I guess that's about the gist of it. Let's go out in the yard and practice where we have a chance of finding something."

Katie stared at him. "Treasure in this yard? In this plain old yard?"

Her father took the handle out of her hand. "I didn't say treasure, I said practice, and I said *something*. There's bound to be metal of some kind even in this plain old yard. After all, there was a house here before we bought this property. Remember? And there was still an old shed right in the corner until your grandmother wanted the space for her rose garden."

Turning on the detector he began walking in a straight line, moving the plate from side to side in wide arcs. Katie stared at the plate, listening to the steady hum. She was not really expecting anything to happen, but it was fascinating just the same.

Suddenly the signal turned into a loud, irregular beep.

"Wow! Wow! Let's dig!" Katie shouted. She ran toward the garden house for a shovel.

Her father was excited too, but he took the shovel from her when she came back. "Hold your horses. We can't just dig up our lawn like you dig over at Frank's. You know your grandmother aims to keep this yard picture pretty."

"You can't let grass stop you when you're looking for treasure."

"Now just wait a minute. According to what the book you brought from the library says, chances are that what we've found is a coin or even a snap tab off a pop can. In which case all we need to do is lift a plug of grass which can be put back."

"A coin? One coin?"

"That's right. And probably a penny at that. Don't you remember reading about that?"

"I didn't pay too much attention about digging for pennies."

He stooped, and exactly where the signal had given its sudden high beep, he cut out a plug of grass with his pocket knife. Sure enough, down among the roots below the plug there was a lone penny, and not even a very old one.

"What would you expect here in our yard?" Katie said.

Her father looked at her impatiently. "You can expect to finds lots of pennies and assorted pieces of metal of no particular value. That's part of the game, whether you like it or not."

She shrugged. "I'm sorry. I won't complain any more. We're just practicing anyhow. Could I have a turn now?"

"Sure. You can have all the turns you want. It's your project and I want you to enjoy it."

Katie rested the detector on the grass and looked at

him. "And you too, Daddy. I hope you enjoy it too."

He gave her a little shove. "Sure I will. I have to admit I'm interested in this gadget and what it might turn up."

"There's absolutely no telling," Katie said. "But something fantastic. That's for sure."

• • ● • •

Katie was awake at six on her birthday, but she made herself stay in bed for a little while. Her father had warned her last night not to wake him up at the crack of dawn. This was going to be a very special day and she didn't plan to do anything to start it off wrong.

She had waited just about as long as she could manage when she heard her father talking to her mother in their bedroom.

Up she popped and in just a minute or two the whole family was up and everybody was excited. Her grandmother cooked breakfast while her mother was dressing to go to the store. Her father was going to take the whole day off to help Katie look for treasure.

They were planning to go to the woods in back of the fort and try for the treasure buried by Captain Blackbeard. Katie shivered whenever she remembered that the cruel old pirate had chained his cabin boy to a tree and then shot him so his ghost could guard the treasure. Katie's father reminded her that you would never find the treasure if you had anything to dig with. But she didn't care. She still insisted they go there first.

She ate a couple of bites of scrambled eggs and a half a piece of toast and then sat watching her father with impatience as he took seconds on eggs and thirds on coffee.

The minute he picked up his napkin to wipe his mouth she pushed back from the table. "Can we go now? Right this minute?"

"Could I maybe brush my teeth?" he asked.

"If you'll hurry. I can get mine done in nothing flat."

He groaned. "Oh, brother. I'm afraid this is going to be a very long day."

"Not long enough for me," she said, heading out the door.

• • ● • •

It was hot and still in the woods back of the fort. The dunes at the edge of the beach and the trees here in the woods blocked the breeze from the river. They were both sweating in a short time and Katie's father said, "I'd be a whale of a lot cooler at the store."

Katie felt a small amount of alarm. "But there's no treasure there."

He laughed. "That's for sure, certainly not the kind you're after. Don't worry, Katie, baby. This is your day and we'll look wherever and as long as you want to. We're bound to find something."

But they didn't. The detector beeped loudly at several points, but when they dug down all they found was old beer cans.

They sat down after a while by a twisted oak tree to put more powdered sulphur on their ankles and inside their belts to help ward off chiggers. Katie still had some itchy places left over from her bites the last time she was in these woods.

Without consciously hearing anything, Katie saw a shadowy movement between the trees. She reached out with a powdery finger to touch her father's arm, glad it was his arm and not just Lorie's.

"What's up?" he asked.

She pointed to where the shadow had been and now wasn't.

"I don't see anything."

"Something moved, Dad. Right there."

"The wind blew a bush."

"What wind?"

"A dog passing by."

"Yeah, probably. I hope."

He laughed. "Or a wildcat."

She moved closer to him and he said, "I was only kidding. If there are wildcats still living out here they're more afraid of us than we are of them. We wouldn't see or hear one, especially in the daytime."

Just then the shadow reappeared among the trees and took form. It was Petey Moon. He came out from among the trees then and walked toward them.

Katie hadn't seen the old man since the day she'd been lost in these woods. He was still dressed in the same hot, dark clothes, and he was still scary looking.

As he came up to them she swallowed hard and then said, "Hi, Petey Moon. Do you remember me? You helped me and my friend get out of these woods when we were lost."

"Humph," was all he said.

"Well, anyway, you did and we appreciated it. Both of us."

He stared at her. "How come you back heah, then?"

Katie's father got up and picked up the detector. "This gadget locates metal in the ground. We're just

96

having a go at seeing what might be buried out here."

"I know what that thing is. I seen 'em before. Folks all the time looking in Petey Moon's woods. Nuthin heah any more 'cept Petey."

Katie scrambled to her feet. "Was there ever anything out here?"

He shrugged his big shoulders. "Maybe so. Maybe not."

Katie's father said, "Pete, in the old days, I mean the real old days before this fort was built, there was another fort and a settlement of houses out here somewhere. Do you know where it was?"

Petey Moon stared at her father a long time, then he said, "Petey knows."

Katie tugged at her father's arm, sure he was getting off the trail of treasure.

He looked at her. "Take it easy, will you? I know it's not what you have in mind, but at a place like that we might find some pretty interesting stuff."

"Like what?" Katie asked, skeptical. "What could we find at a place like that?"

"Oh, medicine bottles. Tools. Old ammunition. Pottery. All kinds of things we never use any more."

"Then why do we want to find them?"

He threw up his hands in exasperation. "Just because they're old. They're a part of our history. They help us know what life was like in the old days. They help us understand and appreciate the people who lived back then."

Katie sighed, sorry she had gotten him riled up. "Well, I guess they are kind of important. They're the small treasure Grandmother was talking about."

"Of course they're important," her father said, turning to Petey Moon again. "Would you take me, or us, there one day? I'd pay you for your time."

Petey Moon shrugged. "Maybe so. Maybe not."

Katie was relieved. They certainly wouldn't be going today.

Her father picked up the detector again, but he clearly didn't have his mind on her treasure. "We'd really need to make a preliminary trip out there," he said. "We'd have to check out the site so we'd know the best places to dig. Maybe there's a book at the library, or some research paper, or even a map we could study. You know, Katie, this could be a great hobby. If I got seriously interested in it I might even start taking some regular time off from the store to pursue it."

Katie's jaw dropped. He was talking about taking off from work again and not even on a birthday. And, she didn't want to press it, but it sounded as if he was talking about taking her along. Now, that had to be really neat!

Petey Moon was moving away from them through the woods.

"I'll get in touch with you," her father called.

"Maybe so. Maybe not," Petey Moon said.

• • ● • •

It was nearly twelve o'clock. No sign of treasure. Not even a pop can.

Mr. Reise wiped his face with his dirty, wet handkerchief. "What say we take a break for lunch and talk about what you want to do next? We could pick up hamburgers and cold drinks at the beach and eat at one of the shaded picnic tables. There'll be a breeze coming up from the ocean, and that's the main thing I could use right now.''

Katie blew out a hot sigh. "Sounds great to me." She had been afraid he might suggest going home.

They drove from the fort area to the beach along a wide road running through the woods just in back of the sand dunes.

Oaks and cedars grew close to the road, shading it with thickly laced branches. Spanish moss hung in long sheaths from the branches. Back from the road Katie could see grape vines as thick as ropes hanging down between the trees.

"I'll bet you could swing on those grape vines just like Tarzan did," Katie said.

Her father glanced over toward the woods and then nodded. "You can. Well, maybe not like Tarzan, but Frank and I used to do it when we were kids. There were some old oaks growing on the river bluff with branches hanging out over the water. We used to climb along the branches and then catch a vine, swing out over the water, and drop in."

Katie sat up straight in her seat. "Could we do that, Dad? That would be super fun."

He grinned. "I couldn't, or wouldn't. But you might if we could find the trees and the vines over the water. Where Frank and I used to go is private property now."

"We could look for another place."

He grinned again. "We could, I guess. Sometime."

Katie hated that word *sometime*. "Please, Daddy, say when."

He sighed. "I can't say when, Katie. I'm a working

man you know." He looked over at her. "One treasure at a time, huh?"

When they hit the main road going out to the ocean, they turned and drove to an open stand to buy hamburgers, cold drinks, and hot apple tarts to take to the picnic grounds.

The beach was full of people, some swimming, some stretched out on brightly colored towels sun bathing, and others sitting at the shaded tables doing away with large quantities of food from fat straw hampers.

A strong breeze blew up from the ocean. The water was deep blue under a clear sky. White-capped breakers rolled in, scattering shells and sometimes people.

In the tiny square of shade made by the lifeguard's stand two girls were sitting. Katie looked quickly to see if Lou Earle was on duty, but he wasn't. Every so often the girls looked up at the lifeguard and then whispered together. He stared out toward the ocean, completely ignoring them.

Katie thought suddenly of Lorie. Whenever Lou Earle was on duty she and Lorie did all their swimming right in front of his guard stand, and spent all their time out of the water very close to it. Lou Earle was the handsomest boy in town and the best swimmer. Katie thought she might marry him some day, though she'd never told that to anyone, not even Lorie.

Katie slowly unpeeled her hamburger from its paper wrapper, missing Lorie. They hadn't done much of anything together lately. It wasn't that they were mad or anything, but they just seemed to be avoiding each other.

Tonight Lorie would be coming for supper, but that

was because Katie's mother had insisted Katie should ask her. Now Katie was glad that she had.

"You're looking pretty serious all of a sudden," her father said. "Your hamburger not big enough or something?"

She shook her head. "I was just thinking of something kind of sad, but I'm okay now." She took a large bite and said with her mouth full, "This is good. I was pretty hungry."

"Me too. Say, do you notice some of these people staring at us? We must look pretty crummy."

Katie leaned forward and whispered fiercely, like a spy in an old television movie. "They'd really stare if they knew we are famous treasure hunters and that we're about to discover the most fantastic treasure the world has ever seen."

She sat back giggling a moment and then she sighed. "Will I ever really find one?"

He looked at her solemnly and then shrugged his shoulders. "Maybe so. Maybe not."

That made her giggle again.

"Anyway, you're having fun looking for one, aren't you?" he asked.

"I'd have a lot better time finding one."

"I don't know. I've heard tell that the fun is in the looking, not the finding." He rolled the paper trash from his lunch into a ball, stuffed it into a bag and handed it to her. "Why don't you clear up for us? And I'll tell you what I'd like to do. I'd like to lie down on top of this table for about ten minutes for a small siesta. Then I'll be ready to get up and go again. Wherever you say."

Katie put all the trash in the big metal can near the table and thought about where she wanted to go next. She didn't really want to go back to the woods near the fort. Not unless they had, as her father said, a specific site to explore.

They could go down on the beach and look for some kind of trail. But today an awful lot of people were out there who would just ask questions and follow them if they did find a trail. Besides, she didn't think her father would want to stay out in the sun in the middle of the day. He'd get more burned than some of those other people lying in the blazing sun.

The best thing to do, and she'd been planning to do it later on anyway, was to go to her uncle Frank's place. That would be a specific site, and although the yard was huge, they had hours. They could cover it all if they went pretty soon.

She stared at her father impatiently.

He looked back from half-opened eyes. "Ahah. I'm afraid you have a plan."

"I do. I do. I certainly do!"

• • ● • •

While they were driving toward her uncle's house, her father said there was no way they could cover the whole yard in one afternoon, but they could certainly make a start.

"Well, we know the treasure was buried in the back end of the yard, so we can start there," Katie said.

He glanced over at her, scowling a little. "The alleged treasure was buried under three trees in a triangle. The trees were cut down long ago, so we don't know anything for sure."

102

"Oh, Daddy, don't be such a pessimist. You've got to have faith if you want to find treasure."

He straightened up. "Who's a pessismist? I've got a shovel handy in the back seat, haven't I?"

They parked in an open stretch of sand near her uncle Frank's kitchen steps. Katie's father got the detector and shovel out of the car and carried them to the back end of the yard. She followed close behind with a hand trowel and a box. She figured they'd turn up a few small things before they found the biggie.

When her father motioned that she was to take the first turn, she grabbed the detector and began pushing it beside the rotting old board fence. The detector started its sharp, high pitched hum almost immediately. Katie stopped, eyes wide.

"Probably just a rusty nail from the fence," her father said.

He was right. Katie dug up a couple of nails lying close together in the roots of a clump of grass. She threw them aside, fussing. "How'll we ever know when we're into the real thing? There could be a million nails along here."

"Right. Looks as if we're going to have to do a lot of digging, but I'm game if you are."

"I'm game; I'm game," she said and, lifting the detector, started moving it along the grass again.

On the first run beside the fence they found twenty-seven nails, and at the end a rusted tin can and a mason jar lid.

Katie was glad to give her father a turn with the detector. It got heavy in a hurry and even in her uncle Frank's yard in the shade it was hot.

Her father started in the corner where she'd stopped, ready to go back across the yard. The detector signaled the presence of metal immediately. Leaning it against the fence he got the shovel and carefully lifted out a large clump of grass and roots. In the sand below they saw a cluster of cans rusted together and a couple of chips of an old china plate.

Looking at Katie he asked, "You know what I think? No, wait, let me just try something."

He moved the detector a few feet away from the fence into the yard, and as soon as he turned the power on, the detector again signaled metal. He shook his head. "Pumpkin, I think what we've got here is an old dump pile, you know, where they used to burn the household trash before garbage trucks came on the scene."

"Oh, Daddy. What a dumb detector!"

He laughed. "No, not dumb. It's just doing what it's supposed to do—find metal. It's not designed to pick and choose. But even here, Katie, according to the things I've read, we could find something interesting, maybe not of any great value, but pretty interesting."

"But that could take the rest of my day and we still wouldn't have searched the yard for the real treasure."

He wiped the sweat off his face with his shirt sleeve and he wasn't laughing any more. "Katie, you're some kind of a stubborn kid, you know that?" Then he handed her the detector. "But you're right. This is your treasure hunt on your birthday. I can rent this thing another time and excavate this trash pile. Today you lead out and we'll look where you want to look."

They did just that. They crisscrossed the whole back

104

yard, stopping only to go for cold drinks. The detector sounded its faithful drone and every so often went into its irregular, high-pitched call. She or her father dug at every one of the signals, but by late afternoon all they had to show for their work was an odd assortment of things—rusty old bottle caps, a brass hinge, a spoon, a half-rotted-through tackle box, and several brass buttons. Hardly what Katie had in mind!

Her father liked everything but the tackle box, which he threw away. Katie tried to like the collection too. After all, her father had taken off a whole day to help her look for treasure. It wasn't his fault they hadn't found one. And she could see he was really worn out.

She tried to sound enthusiastic when they got in the car to go home. "Well, we did find some kind of neat stuff anyway. I appreciate your getting the detector and helping me look."

"My pleasure. Anything for the birthday girl. And cheer up. It's still your birthday and you've got cake and ice cream and maybe even a present or two coming up."

"That's right!" she said, feeling a whole lot better. "Presents are always neat."

7 · A Super Day

Katie's mother and grandmother were sitting out on the patio when Katie and her father got home. Rushing to get in the house, Katie gave them only a quick, "Hi."

"Any luck?" her mother called.

"Dad will tell you," Katie called back. From the kitchen door she could see what she was looking for. A tall white cake was sitting on the breakfast room table. It was covered with pink flowers and curling green leaves, and had pink and green candles on top.

Sitting next to it were two wrapped packages with bows on top and what looked like a birthday card. Running in to the table she snatched up the card. It had a foreign stamp on it, and her name in her uncle's angular black script.

Looking up at her grandmother who was coming in with place mats for the table, she said, "Uncle Frank sent me a card all the way from Mexico!" She weighed it in her hand. "It probably has money in it. Can I open it and my presents now?"

"Don't you want to wait until after supper and the big cake cutting? Lorie will be here then, too."

Katie thought it over. Opening several presents at the same time was fun. She sighed. "I guess I could wait."

Her grandmother laughed. "I believe you actually are getting older. Why don't you take a shower before Lorie comes. Wash off a few pounds of that Florida sand?"

Katie looked down at herself. "I collected more dirt and little buggy creatures than I did treasure."

Her grandmother put an arm around her. "It was fun, though, wasn't it? Your daddy said he had fun."

Katie nodded. "Yeah, it was fun." She headed out the door and then looked back. "But I'm still going to find a treasure, you know."

"I believe you," her grandmother said.

• • ● • •

Lorie arrived just as supper was ready to go on the table, so the two girls didn't have time to say more than a few words. This suited Katie, who was feeling just a little uneasy where Lorie was concerned.

Lorie handed Katie a heavyish oblong package and Katie said, "Thanks, Lorie," and added it to the other packages on the table.

They all sat down then and bowed their heads to say the blessing together.

Come, Lord Jesus.
Be our guest.
Share these gifts
Which thou hast blessed. Amen.

Before they raised their heads, Katie's father continued, "And we ask Your special blessings on Katie, Lord. We thank You for her and pray that she will have many, many happy years under your loving-watch care. Amen."

Katie looked up as her mother put a heaping plate in front of her. "First plate for the birthday girl!"

"Boy, this looks great," Katie said, wondering if she had to wait until everyone was served. There was bar-bequed chicken, yellow rice, and creamy cole slaw with carrot sticks on the side.

She picked up her fork. "Just a minute, Katie," her mother said.

• • ● • •

"Now for the presents!" Katie cried, finishing off her last bite of cake.

She opened the one from her parents first. It was a transistor radio. Katie's eyes widened. "Thanks, Mom and Dad. You didn't have to get me anything, not after renting the detector and taking me out for the day and all."

Her father said, "We thought you might like one for company on some of your extended travels over the island." He cleared his throat. "Which we naturally hope will be on an authorized level."

"Naturally," she said, beginning on her grandmother's gift. Inside the box, wrapped in tissue, was a blue leather Bible with Katie's name stamped in gold.

Katie took it out of the box carefully. "Thank you very much, Grandmother. I never had one this nice. I'll take real good care of it."

"Well, I want you to do that, but I hope you'll use it, too. Read and study it."

Katie handed it to her mother to look at. "Sure I will." She tossed her head. "I'll probably read it through a couple of times before my next birthday."

"That's my girl," her father said.

Lorie's gift was two mystery books and Katie hadn't read either one. She clapped her hands together over them. "Thanks a lot, Lorie. You know just what I like."

Lorie had been waiting with an anxious expression on her face and now she relaxed. "You're welcome. I'm glad you like them."

"And now for Uncle Frank's card," Katie said, tearing the envelope open carefully so as not to ruin the bright orange and white stamp. In the envelope was a flowered card with a printed birthday greeting, and a note folded inside the card. Katie rechecked the envelope and peered between the two halves of the card to be sure there wasn't any money tucked away. There wasn't. She was embarrassed then that she'd done such a thing and, hurriedly opening the note, she read it aloud.

"Dear Niece Katie, sorry I'm not there for your birthday, but I'm sending this card early to be sure to reach you in time. I want you to know that one of the first things I did when we made port in Mexico was to go ashore and buy you a Mexican fiesta dress. I thought you'd like to have it to wear for your special program at church."

Katie stopped reading long enough to say, "Wow! What a great present!" Then she read on.

"I guess I'll have to go to church now myself to see you in it."

Katie looked up and grinned at her father.

"Well, it's a start," he said.

She nodded and read the rest of the note. "Eat an extra piece of cake for me and have a great birthday. See you soon. Love, Uncle Frank."

"What a thoughtful thing for Frank to do," her mother said, getting up to begin clearing the table.

"You're lucky," Lorie said. "I have to wear Mrs. Bailey's Japanese kimono that's a million years old." She leaned over and whispered to Katie, "Now show me what you found today. On your treasure hunt."

Katie reluctantly got up to get the box of things she and her father had found. She guessed what Lorie was going to say, and she was right.

"Wowie!" Lorie said. "You really uncovered a Spanish gold mine, didn't you?"

"Well, it's pretty good stuff, even if it isn't gold," Katie said, feeling as if she had to defend her father. "I'm starting a collection of old things like this. They're part of our history, you know." Until this minute she hadn't thought of starting such a collection, but now it seemed like a good idea.

She picked up one of the buttons and polished it against the leg of her jeans. "This needs cleaning with brass polish. And wait until this hinge is shined up. No telling what it came off of—a really long time ago."

Lorie picked up a button and turned it over in her fingers, examining it closely. It was small and rounded over like a tiny mushroom.

"This is kind of interesting stuff," she said grudgingly. "I can just see this button on a little old lady's high collar." She put the button back in the box. "It would make a pretty good hobby to collect things like this. I could get into it myself. Probably."

Katie put down the box and hugged her friend. "Sure you could. We could work on it together. There must be all kinds of places we could look for old stuff like this."

Her grandmother had stopped to listen to the girls. "There are," she said, "even without digging up the state of Florida. Flea markets sometimes have this kind of thing and junk stores. As a matter of fact, one of my new friends at church owns the junk store on Eighteenth Street. I've been wanting to go out there. Why don't the three of us go out tomorrow and just see what there is to see?"

"You want to, Lorie?" Katie asked excitedly.

"Sure I do. That would be fun."

"Thanks, Grandmother," Katie said and looked back at Lorie. "And when I get my detector we can look at the beach and in the parks and even in our own yards for buried stuff." She took a deep breath. "And then when we're old enough we can go looking for any kind of treasure we want, anywhere on this island and in faraway mysterious places! Daddy says so. Right, Daddy?"

"Right," he said. "Why not?"

• • ● • •

Lorie had to go home soon after supper. Katie found herself too excited to settle down to watch TV or to start reading one of her new books. It wasn't even dark outside yet.

There ought to be something else to do to finish out her birthday in a fun way.

"Why don't you get some paper towels or an old cloth and go out and clean up the metal detector," her father said. "I have to take it back first thing in the morning."

That wasn't exactly what Katie had in mind, but she nodded. Getting a cloth from her grandmother, she went out on the patio where the detector was sitting.

As she polished away at the metal surfaces of the control box, some of her excitement faded, leaving her with a feeling of being both happy and sad at the same time. It had been great to go treasure hunting with her dad, but it would have been greater to find something really special. You just couldn't call an old hinge really special, in spite of what she'd said to Lorie.

Getting up from her chair she carried the detector over to the side of the yard. She just might make another run or two before pitch dark. After all, somebody did have a house on this lot a long time ago, just as her father said. There could be about anything right along this row of shrubs.

By the time she'd walked a few feet, she was really excited again, convinced she was going to find something all by herself and that it was going to be special.

Nothing disturbed the steady beep from the coil as it slid along the ground, but she knew it was just a matter of time. She got up to her grandmother's prize rose garden in the corner of the yard, hesitated just a moment, and then eased in between the shrubs and the sticky arms of the rosebushes. She couldn't stop now.

At that moment the detector went into its high-pitched, irregular beep, signaling metal below the extended branches of a bush covered with brilliant red roses.

This was it! It had to be. She was about to find her special birthday treasure! She leaned the detector into the shrubbery and ran for the garden shed to get the shovel. She was going to dig up whatever was hiding there and surprise everybody.

Coming back, she stopped at the edge of the rose bed, worried for the first time about what she was going to do. Could she dig without cutting into the roots of the rosebush and maybe killing it? Her grandmother was mighty particular about her rose bed, fertilizing and spraying and cutting off the blooms just at the right part of the stem.

Katie started forward again. Nobody could expect her not to dig up her treasure once she'd found it.

Then she stopped and slowly backed out of the rose garden. "I can't just go in there and dig. I'll have to ask her permission."

She sank down on the grass, so frustrated she thought she might burst out crying. "She'll never give me permission. Not in a million years."

● ● ● ● ●

There was quite a family discussion about the matter. Her father said, "Now Katie, be reasonable. You know from experience that just a scrap of old metal or a penny could be setting off the signal. You wouldn't want to risk that nice bush for something like that."

"But I just know it's something special this time."

"You felt the same way every other time today," he said.

114

"No, Daddy, no, I really didn't."

Her mother said, "But Katie B., all that ground was dug up when Mamma put in the roses. If anything had been there, the man helping her would have found it when he was digging."

"Maybe not," Katie reasoned. "Billy Mack was the one helping her, and you always say Billy Mack just does what he has to do to get by. He probably stopped digging just before where my treasure is."

"You may have something there," her mother said, laughing a little. Then she was serious again. "Even so, you can't dig around that bush without cutting into its root system. You might even kill it."

"I know that or I wouldn't have come in to ask."

"Oh, my goodness," her grandmother said. "I'd certainly not like you to dig up my rose garden."

"Well, that settles it," her father said. "Katie, you'll have to let this one go. You've got plenty of other places to dig."

"Now, wait a minute," her grandmother said. "I didn't say she couldn't dig, I said I wouldn't like it. But, maybe if it's not too close to a bush and she dug very carefully there wouldn't be any problem." She paused. "You know, I'm with Katie on this. I have a feeling she's found something really special this time."

• • ● • •

They all went out in the yard together. Katie's father had suggested they wait until early in the morning, but Katie said that this was really a birthday treasure and it had to be dug for on the very day of her birthday.

"Just to be on the safe side, why don't I check it out

115

with the detector and then do the digging," her father said.

Pushing the detector in front of him, he squeezed along between the roses and the hedge. In seconds the signal went off, right under the red rosebush. He turned and looked at Katie's grandmother, his eyebrows raised.

Katie swallowed, trying to accept what she believed was coming. Her grandmother was going to say it wasn't possible to dig this close without hurting the bush, and to just please bring the detector out of her garden.

She tried to tell herself that the detector was probably above a stupid penny, but she didn't believe it. It was more than a penny. It had to be.

Her grandmother picked up the shovel and handed it to her father. "Start digging next to the shrubbery and work toward the bush. Maybe you can come in sideways without cutting up too many roots."

"Just a minute," he said. "Why don't I take out a plug first, just where the signal indicated metal. We may find a coin and that will be easy to get out."

Katie held her breath while he lifted a plug out of the mulch over the roots. Sand and rotted mulch fell loose as he did and there was no coin.

Katie breathed again in relief. Then he pushed the knife into the ground as deep as it would go. "There's something here," he said. "I feel it."

Katie picked up the shovel this time. "Dig! Dig!"

He dug in sideways with the shovel, trying to get in and under whatever had set off the detector.

After a few minutes he said, "I'm under something,

116

whether it's a big root or Katie's treasure, I don't know."

"Can you see anything?" Katie asked, crowding in closer.

"No, and you stay back out of my way, unless of course you want me to get stabbed to death by this rosebush." He lifted another shovel full of sand and roots and put it aside.

Then he got down on his hands and knees. "Wait a minute, fellas. Here's something interesting."

"What? What?" Katie cried, pressing in on him again.

He was feeling in the dirt with his fingers and brushing sand away from something. "It's too dark for me to see, but it feels like a little chest or something."

"A chest!" Katie cried. "A pirate chest?"

He was working with both hands. "I don't think so, but it's a little box of some kind all right."

In another few minutes he had it out and was handing it to Katie. "Wow! What is it?" she squealed.

The little chest was made of wood, with strips of metal banded around it. The wood was rotted and caving in at several places, and the metal was rusted and sagging.

Her grandmother said, "Why it looks like a little doll trunk. I've seen them at antique shows."

"A doll trunk!" Katie cried, not sure she liked that idea. She sat down on the grass and put it between her knees. "Anyway, let's get it open and see what's inside."

The latch on the side was rusted completely together. There was no way she could get it open.

Her father said, "Wait a few minutes until I can fill this hole with dirt and put the hose on it to soak. Then we'll take your find into the kitchen where we can see what we're doing. I'll probably have to use a screwdriver to pry it open."

"Oh, I can't wait!" Katie wailed, and then, looking at her grandmother and her grandmother's rosebush, she said, "I mean, I can hardly wait."

Her grandmother and mother had been talking quietly and now her mother said, "Katie, don't get your hopes up too high. You know, some child could have buried a pet in the little trunk."

"Oh, mother! Gross!"

"I'm sorry," her mother said. "I just didn't want you to open it and find something that might upset you."

Katie picked up the chest and took it to the patio steps to wait. She knew it wasn't going to have any old bones or anything dumb like that in it.

Her father had to bring extra soil to fill in the hole next to the rosebush. Her grandmother pulled the soaker over and began laying it next to the bush to water down the disturbed ground, and Katie waited. It was getting pretty dark.

After what seemed like a terribly long time, they were finished. Her father got a screwdriver out of the garden shed and, coming over to her, said, "Let's go in to the light. You run in and put some newspaper on the kitchen table and we'll work from there."

Standing in the kitchen, he turned the little trunk over and over in his hands. "Hmmm, it has to be real old. You know, there was a shed in that corner of the

118

yard when we bought this property, so this had to have been buried before the shed was built.''

Her mother said, "I guess that's why it didn't rot away completely. The shed gave it some protection.''

"Well, just open it, open it!" Katie said.

Almost as soon as he began to pry with the screwdriver at the latch, it fell apart. The hinges at the back were as badly rusted, and gave way easily, too.

"Too bad we couldn't save these old fittings," he said.

"Open it, open it!" Katie cried.

"You open it," he said and put it down on the table in front of her.

Looking at the three of them, she crossed her fingers then began to work at the lid. It didn't come right open and at one point her father had to pry a little. Then the lid was off and she laid it aside.

The trunk was not filled with gold and jewels the way she'd seen in pictures. But she wasn't really expecting that, so she wasn't disappointed. But there was something inside, something wrapped in a cloth. The cloth looked like pink-striped flannel, but it had turned almost brown and was spotted with darker brown stains. She looked at her grandmother, thinking of the bones. "Shall I unwrap it?"

"I can hardly wait," her grandmother said.

Katie lifted the small bundle. It was light and knobby. It is bones, she thought first, feeling gingerly along it with her fingers. Then her eyes widened in surprise. It felt like a doll. It couldn't be. Who'd bury a doll?

She laid the bundle on the table and began peeling

119

back the cloth. And then she stopped and stared. It was a doll. A china doll about as long as her hand, with painted blue eyes and a smiling pink mouth.

It was wearing a long white dress, which had turned a light, spotty brown, and two petticoats, all trimmed with lace. Yellow curls peeped out from under a tiny crocheted cap.

"My goodness, Katie, what a beautiful little doll," her grandmother said.

"I know," Katie said, "I know." She lifted the petticoats higher to see the tiny body and then she knew why the doll had been buried. "She's all broken," Katie cried.

Her grandmother sat down beside her at the table, and they looked at the doll together. "It's a shame," her grandmother said. "The little girl who owned her must have dropped her and, of course, these bisque dolls do break easily." She moved the pieces of the doll's body around. "It looks as if the pieces are all here, the biggest ones anyway. We could take her to the doll hospital in Jacksonville and have her mended."

"Oh, could we?" Katie cried. "Could we really?"

"We can certainly try. And while she's there I'll show you how to soak these little clothes to whiten them. You're lucky to find a doll with the original clothes."

Katie had started out the door to find a box for the doll when she heard her mother say, "It really is a nice little doll. Too bad she's broken. She'd be a lot more valuable if she were whole."

● ● ● ● ●

120

Katie was sitting at her desk. She had restudied the catalogue that her father had brought home. Then she had circled with red crayon the model they'd agreed was the best one for her to buy. She figured it would take her nearly a year to save the money she'd need, but her father was already planning to rent a detector for them to work with in the meantime. So she guessed she could wait.

And then she'd read a whole chapter from her new Bible. She really was going to read it all the way through, at least once, before her next birthday. She ran her fingers over the smooth blue leather of the Bible and then folded her hands over it. Usually she said her prayers after she had gotten into bed and sometimes she fell asleep before she was even finished. But tonight she was feeling pretty grown up, sitting at her desk with her new Bible. She wanted to pray right here while she was wide awake and could think of what she was saying to God.

"Thank you for my family, dear God, and bless everybody in it. Especially bless Uncle Frank and keep him safe, and thank you that he's bringing me a Mexican dress and going to church for my special program. And thank you that Lorie and I are best friends again, and that Grandma is going to take us to the junk store tomorrow. And especially thank you for letting me find the little doll. Amen."

Opening her eyes she pulled the shoe box holding the baby doll close and touched the little face. "I think you are valuable even all broken," she said softly. "You are very, very valuable to me, just like you were to the first girl you belonged to."

Katie began to picture that other girl. She saw her in a long brown dress with a white lace collar and high top black shoes with buttons up the side. She had blond curls like Lorie's but long ones, down around her shoulders, and she had a big plaid bow ribbon on top, holding back her curls.

Katie wondered how she happened to break the doll, and how long she cried. Maybe she had a brother who pushed her and then turned around and helped her give the doll a decent burial.

Katie felt sad about all of that. She leaned over and touched the tiny baby face. "When you are all mended I'm going to put you up in my doll cabinet so you'll never get broken again."

She sighed. "I have to give you a new name since I don't know what the other girl called you. Of course, it has to be a special name." She thought a minute and then sat upright in her chair. "I know. I'll name you Mary Ruth Bradbury after my grandmother. After all, I couldn't have found you if she hadn't let me dig in her rose garden. Besides, that name just suits you."

Her mother called from the living room. "Katie, time you were in bed."

"Okay, Mamma, I'm going." She got up from her desk. "Goodnight, Mary Ruth. Sleep tight! Don't let the skeeters bite."

The baby doll seemed very little and alone in the shoe box. Katie looked over at her rag doll waiting on her pillow. Katie had slept with Lady Jane since the day her grandmother Reise had finished making her.

She hesitated only a minute. Then she went over and brought Lady Jane back, and laid her next to the

122

baby doll. "Now, you're not by yourself," she said. "Goodnight, Lady Jane! Goodnight, Mary Ruth Bradbury!"

Turning off her light, Katie jumped into bed. She lay quietly in the darkness, but she certainly wasn't very sleepy.

What in the world was the junk store like inside? She'd seen the outside with the old refrigerators and bed frames and wooden chairs stacked all around. The window sills were filled with pieces of china and glass vases. The inside of the store looked dark, and riding by you could just get a glimpse of long aisles stretched back between counters and shelves full of all kinds of mysterious stuff.

Katie sat up straight in her bed. In the middle of all that wonderful junk she was going to find some kind of treasure!

"Wow!" she said out loud, and laid back on her pillow. She shut her eyes tight. She would make herself go to sleep.

Tomorrow was going to be another super day.